BEST
FRIENDS
THROUGH
ETERNITY

BEST
FRIENDS
THROUGH
ETERNITY

SYLVIA McNICOLL

TUNDRA BOOKS

Published in Canada by Tundra Books,
a division of Random House of Canada Limited,
One Toronto Street, Suite 300, Toronto, Ontario M5C 2V6

Published in the United States by Tundra Books of Northern New York,
P.O. Box 1030, Plattsburgh, New York 12901

Library of Congress Control Number: 2014934268

Library and Archives Canada Cataloguing in Publication

McNicoll, Sylvia, 1954-, author
Best friends through eternity / Sylvia McNicoll.

Issued in print and electronic formats.
ISBN 978-1-77049-710-8 (bound).—ISBN 978-1-77049-712-2 (epub)

I. Title.

PS8575.N52B47 2015   JC813'.54   C2014-900835-X
                                               C2014-900836-8

Edited by Sue Tate
Designed by Rachel Cooper
The text was set in Garamond.
www.tundrabooks.com

Printed and bound in the United States of America

1 2 3 4 5 6   20 19 18 17 16 15

For Bob, my best friend through eternity

ACKNOWLEDGMENTS

All kinds of support was needed for the creation of this work, and I am extremely grateful to the Ontario Arts Council (Writers in Reserve) and the Canada Council (Creative Writing Grant) for funding the research and writing time necessary for this novel.

A huge thank-you goes to Becky Dumais and her chosen daughters, Sophia and Grace, for sharing their stories of finding each other. Reading *Message from an Unknown Chinese Mother: Stories of Loss and Love* by Xinran helped me understand some of the emotions behind international adoption.

Thank you to Beena Patel for consulting and supplying anecdotes and information on East Indian culture. Much appreciation goes to Dr. Sarah Miyata-Kane, who volunteered at the Body Worlds exhibit in the Ontario Science Centre and helped many, including me, understand what a lung feels like. She also gave insight into the kind of character Paige would be and recommended reading *Stiff: The Curious Lives of Human Cadavers* by Mary Roach, which I, in turn, recommend to you, if you have a strong stomach. Thanks also to my test readers, Michelle Fornasier and Dharma Patel; applause for an early draft certainly supported me emotionally and carried me through in the final writing.

∞

Monday after School

∞ •

Iblame Jasmine for the fact that I'm dying. On Monday afternoon, she should be volunteering in the library. That's what she tells her parents, after all. But, instead, she's sneaking around with Cameron in the mall three blocks from school.

She's probably holding his hand, nuzzling his neck or even kissing him, and who can blame her? He's a good-looking boy, baby-faced with a cleft chin, slow, measuring brown eyes and a generous mouth. His hair is a light shade of milk chocolate, and it has a gentle wave. There isn't a girl in school who doesn't want to go out with him. Including me.

A week ago, I was thrilled that Jazz could snatch Cameron from Vanessa during their monthly breakup drama. Vanessa is the resident volleyball queen, a blonde, hazel-eyed power girl. What a victory! Geeks over jocks, 2–1. Gives everyone hope, even me. Someday I, Paige Barta, might be able to score the best-looking boy out from under one of the long legs of the fair-skinned girls. And really, like Vanessa, I believed the relationship was very temporary. For one thing, Jazz's parents won't let her go out with boys—and not just until she turns fifteen or sixteen. Not ever. For another, she likes books and theater, not ball games on big screens. In an instant Cameron would make up with Vanessa, and we'd be the brainy duo again.

But a week later it already feels like an eternity. Here I am by myself again, shutting down the computers that were left on by the last class. Jazz ditching me, and even using me as a smoke screen for Cameron, has gotten really old.

And it isn't the first time I've been abandoned for the sake of a boy.

Back in China, my birth parents gave me up because the state wouldn't allow them to have more than one child. They needed a boy to carry on the name and the duties of the farm. Like girls can't do that. Still, there's a happy ending to that story. I was "chosen" by my adoptive parents, as they like to tell me.

No one chooses to adopt me as their new lunch or after-school buddy when Jazz abandons me. In fact, in gym class, Vanessa's supporters shove me around, whapping me with balls and snapping wet towels at me, as though I have anything to do with the Great Romance.

I sigh. Two banks of computers—most of them left for me to look after. How many times does the teacher have to tell the morons to save and shut down? I quit the windows as quickly as possible without even looking, pressing "No" to saving changes. Some people will lose their essays and notes, but really, why should I take the time to check which version and file name they need to keep, if *they* can't be bothered?

Third to last computer, Vanessa McDonald's Facebook photo catches my eye. She's puckering her lips and blowing a kiss in it. Her hair looks golden and windblown, her hazel eyes liquid and secretive. The photo makes her look like a model, way better than how she looks on the volleyball court, all red-faced and frizzy-haired.

I skim through the messages, finger hovering over the "Enter" key, ready to close. Her friends seem to have two modes: one, sickly sweet . . .

Kierstead Compo: Ur so purty Van.

Vanessa McDonald: Aw! Luv u 2 Kbear.

Laura Gingham: Best friends 4ever. Can't wait till we get an apartment together.

Kierstead Compo: It's gonna be party heaven!

And the other mode, psycho evil . . .

Morgan Pellam: Saw Cameron sucking face with the Bollywood Biatche.

Kierstead Compo: Can't believe he would dump purty Van for her.

Vanessa McDonald: Bollywood has 2 pay.

Keirstead Compo: Let's get her after school. Make Jasmine a hazbin. LOL

Morgan Pellam: Yeah! Let's surprise Hazbin at the overpass. Rip off her face.

Laura Gingham: Knock out her teeth.

Vanessa McDonald: What about Banana?

Keirstead Compo: Let's take her down, too.

Four little thumbs-up icons show that Gwyn, Emma, Zoe and Rebecca like this.

I'm Banana.

My mouth goes papery dry. Yellow on the outside, a reference to my Asian looks—although I prefer to think my skin has more of a golden hue—white on the inside, referring to the fact that I am being raised Caucasian. I can't speak Mandarin or Cantonese, not that Mom hasn't tried to send me to class. I don't even know what to choose at the Chinese buffet.

Jasmine and I still meet at four-thirty in the parking lot to walk home together. Even though Jasmine says it's our girl time—since she spends the rest of her life with Cameron—it's really so her parents won't suspect. They're Hindus the way mine are Catholics, not that serious or strict about observing all the details. Still, Jasmine certainly isn't supposed to be "sucking face" with a boy, as Morgan so quaintly puts it.

What to do? I squint out the library window. Through the inky black, I can make out white. Like clumps of soggy cloud, the snow drops heavy and fast.

The sky is falling. I swallow hard. In class, with a teacher around, Vanessa's team managed to shove me into the wall, hit me in the face with a ball and trip me. What will happen without any adults around?

"Certainly coming down out there," Mrs. Falkner, our librarian, says. "Maybe you should head home, Paige. We can shelve the books tomorrow."

It's four o'clock on a Monday afternoon. Too early for Jazz to come back. I text her but doubt she even looks at her cell phone when she's with him. If I leave now, I won't be able to warn her in person. What good will a warning do, anyway? Like a pack of hyenas, they'll track us down sometime when no one is around. I lick my teeth . . . smooth. I like the way they look since the braces came off. I don't really want to chance having them kicked in.

If I leave now, no one will be on my tail. I'm not their prime target, anyway. If I don't hang with Jazz, I'll be safe. "Yeah, I'm going to pack up and head home." I snap the last computer off and rush out to my locker. I throw on my coat and shove my hat down over my head, flipping the hood over it. Vanessa's gang needs to have memorized my clothing to know it's me. But the way their eyes take hold of us when we walk down the halls, I don't doubt they have. I kick my sneakers into the locker, pull on my boots and grab my backpack. I won't walk our regular route in case those girls catch up with me somehow.

Instead, I'll take the shortcut along the track. My house backs onto the city of Burlington's railway line, so I know the schedule pretty well. The four-thirty GO Train shouldn't be by for another half an hour, maybe later because of all the snow. By that time, with any luck, I'll be sipping hot chocolate over my algebra.

I duck out and see Mr. Brewster, my science teacher, brushing off his car. He's a cool guy—should I ask him for help? What can he do? Will he drive me out to look for Jazz? That has to be breaking some school board rule. Besides, he can't give us a lift home all the time, can't guard us every moment of the day. I don't wave or call hello, I just scuttle out of the parking lot.

I trudge through the snowdrifts covering the sidewalk. Houses line the streets here; I should be safe. Still, I move quickly and, when someone calls out from behind me, I fall down, instantly covering my head with my arms.

"Hey, Paige, you okay?" a guy in a tuque asks. When his face appears right in front of mine, I stare into his smiling brown eyes. It's Max Liu, the Chinese guy from science class.

"Peachy," I answer. Max being Asian is enough to bug me, enough for me to want to avoid him. His looking amused at me right now makes me want to shove him into the snow.

His friend reaches his hand out to help me up, but I scramble to my feet by myself.

"Didn't mean to startle you like that," Max says.

"Of course not." I raise an eyebrow.

"Sorry." He shrugs and they continue on, laughing and jostling each other.

Down the street, a plow flashes its alien blue lights as it pushes the snow into piles along the side. Piles you could easily stuff a body in, there has already been so much snow this winter. "Wait up, Max!" I call, but he doesn't seem to hear. I wish I could just get over myself and chase after him. Safer. It isn't his fault he's Chinese—or a boy, for that matter.

I jog for a block, but then my feet slide out on some hidden ice and I crash-land on my butt again. I look around. No one chuckles or laughs. I'm alone. *Good.* When I get up, I walk slower, checking over my shoulder for movement or shadows, anything to hint that one of the volleyball girls is stalking me.

I glance toward the road Jasmine and Cameron may come down. If I see them, I can warn her. But it's still too early for her to return, unless she uses her brain and comes back early on account of the storm. I can slow down and wait. Maybe Cameron can walk with us, tell those girls to back off and leave us alone. But Jazz doesn't usually use her head when she hangs around with Cameron.

And I do not wait.

I hear a dog barking at me from behind a picture window, and I keep moving. All I want is to make it to the crossing on Appleby Street and turn onto the gravel along-side the track. No one will see me walking. Those girls won't catch me there. They are planning to catch Jazz at the overpass, not hunt for me. I won't have to stand up for the best friend who has abandoned me for the cleft-chinned brown-eyed boy.

Blinking the snowflakes from my eyes, I duck my head into the wind. Not far now. I make sure the tracks look clear. They have to clean them quickly for the commuter traffic.

I turn onto one of the sets of tracks. On either side of them, a six-foot-high chain-link fence blocks animals and kids from dashing across. People don't understand that trains can't stop like cars. For their average driving speed, trains need the length of sixty railroad cars to stop, Dad told me. If an engineer brakes with less space than that, the whole train derails and chances are whatever is on the track still gets creamed.

I should be safe now. No one will look for me here. Huge drifts fill the gaps between the two sets of tracks and the chain-link fence, so I have no choice but to walk dead center between two metal rails. I sigh, take out my iPod and plug my earbuds in. Trouble is, Jazz and I created the mix together BC (before Cameron), and the first songs in the shuffle are her pick. Soft, sentimental love songs that kind of make me want to stuff snow down her neck so she'll wake up. I know she wanted a boyfriend, needed one really, to prove to herself she's beautiful enough to fit in.

We both have this straight black hair that can't do anything but lie flat. I have a round face, with typical Asian dark eyes. Virtually no eyebrows, but I hide that by wearing black horn-rimmed glasses. Jazz has caterpillar brows that she plucks like crazy, but beneath them she has these incredible pale green eyes and a narrow face. Jazz is beautiful. She doesn't need Cameron to prove that. But to really feel like you belong, a boyfriend like him means everything. For me, too.

I forward ahead on the iPod till I hit a loud, pulsing, hip-hop song. My choice, yeah. I swear the beat rumbles through my feet—great stuff. I walk faster. The wind picks up and drives the snow against my face. I live four long blocks down the track. Not far in good weather. It's just the snow stings now and the wind pushes hard against me. I can imagine that it's Vanessa shoving me against the gym wall.

Is that thunder? I hesitate for a second. Is there even lightning in the winter? All kinds of strange weather seem to be happening with the climate warming. Maybe the rumble is in the music. The next song is one both Jazz and I like: techno rock.

I think of her and wince. How will she make out alone? Could the two of us have stood up to those girls? No way. Not if all ten of them show up at the overpass. Sometimes it's even worse having a witness to your humiliation. I text her again: *Stay away from the overpass.*

The beat crackles like lightning. The drum thumps hard and quick. Have to hand it to the music people, they really take creative risks. I hear the wind howling in between the crackles, which sounds really cool.

Alone against ten, how bad will it get for Jazz?

Only another block to go. The tracks themselves shake. What a storm!

Jasmine all alone.

My watch says 4:10. I face slightly away from the wind and see a light from the corner of my eye. This is nuts. There's still time to head her off. I turn around.

A train throws sparks from the rail not one car length away.

I scream and jump.

Monday at the Beach

∞

When I wake up, I'm standing on a sandy beach by the ocean. Puffy white clouds dot the baby-blue sky. Waves of turquoise water lap gently at the vanilla-colored sand.

My toes dig in, and the hot sugar texture feels good against my feet. The sunshine warms the air blowing gently off the sea. Palm trees, like long-necked ladies, shake their feathery green hair out in the breeze.

This is my kind of heaven.

A tiny figure kneels near the water: a little girl. She wears a one-piece red bathing suit spotted with black to look like a ladybug, and she scoops sand from a hole. She looks so small and alone, something makes me want to protect her, to hug her. Everyone starts as these sweet innocent children. Too bad little kids have to grow up into obnoxious jerks. Ones that snap towels in other people's faces.

I sigh. Something about her seems familiar, tugs at me. Affection? Something I don't feel a lot of for little kids. But I had a bathing suit like that once. Is it those shiny black pigtails, so perky and cheerful-looking? I used to wear my hair like that, too.

She turns my way and smiles, a gap-toothed grin, her cheeks swallowing her eyes till they are happy slits. She looks like . . . like me when I was seven years old. I feel sorry for that person from long ago. She was so lonely. I walk toward her.

"Hi, Paige," she says and stands up, reaching out her arms. "I'm so glad to see you!"

"You can't be . . . ," I start and shake my head. No more eating chocolate bars before going to bed.

"It's me, Kim. Come on. You don't remember your best friend?" She stands up and hugs me now, squeezing tightly.

"Wow. I can't believe I'm dreaming about you." I hug and squeeze back. Normally, that would wake me. You can't hold on to a dream person and feel solid flesh touching you.

"You're not dreaming," she says. There's a hint of melody in the tones she uses as she talks. Singsong, little-kid-speak. But, at seven, people said we were both already such old souls.

"I must be dreaming." I pinch myself a couple of times. "You moved away seven years ago." When I don't wake up, I squint at her suspiciously. "I never got to say good-bye." The strange tug of warmth toward this little girl becomes something that sparks and crackles inside of me.

Her smile turns sad. "That's because I died that summer."

"No!" It's like a fist punches into my stomach. I double over and can't breathe for a moment. But then random memories fly together, making sudden clear sense. My parents never told me much when Kim supposedly moved away. They never suggested e-mailing or writing to her, certainly not visiting. What Kim says has to be true. When I can breathe again, the crackles snap white and hot. "Why did my parents lie?"

"Santa Claus, the Tooth Fairy, the Easter Bunny—do adults ever tell the truth to kids?" Kim's childish singsong voice contrasts with her sad, old-soul thoughts.

My voice lifts a pitch, and I sound more like the little kid now. "How did you die?"

She shrugs her shoulders. "I was sick in the hospital awhile."

This all feels so weird, like a nightmare that spits ugly true things into your sleep. "Why can't I wake up? This is scaring me."

"You are awake, silly. It's just that you're mostly dead now."

My mouth drops, every thought evaporating through it.

Kim frowns as she watches my face. "You need to get used to all this." Then she brightens again. "I know. Wanna help me dig to China?" She doesn't wait for an answer, just drops down on her knees and begins scooping sand from her hole again. "Maybe we can find our real parents."

Despite all logic, the "real parents" we used to hope to find were kings and queens who would be ecstatic to be reunited again. We always dug at holes like that together.

Just like me, Kim is a Chinese orphan adopted by a Canadian family. Her parents and mine discovered each other at a Red Thread meeting, a kind of meet and greet for adopted Chinese kids and their parents. When they saw how well we got along, they began planning playdates and other outings so we could be together. This way we would feel less alone in our new home. The playdates turned into sleepovers and the outings into holidays, until we were inseparable. Her parents became my uncle Jack and my auntie Bev.

Until that summer.

"I can't stay, Kim. I have to get home. Mom will be worried."

Kim looks up at me, tilting her head in a question. "I thought you missed me."

"Seven years ago, sure." I couldn't eat or sleep at the time. My parents bought me a hamster to keep me company till I made a new friend, but I never liked it. Just used it for scientific experiments—timing its treadwheel jaunts, weighing it, putting it through mazes.

"Your mom will get used to you leaving, too. My parents did."

"Stop this. I don't believe you!" I snap.

She pats the sand next to her. "Sit a minute. I'll show you."

When I'm down beside her, she points to the hole in the

sand. It fills with water, just like they always do. She swirls her hand in the liquid mud, and suddenly it becomes a snowy darkness that fills my sight line. I hear a train blasting its horn, wheels grinding and screeching along tracks. I can make out its form, see the green-and-white logo. Bright orange sparks flash through the darkness.

A person walks in front of that train and I holler, "Get out of the way!"

The person wears my winter jacket and hat. She turns for a moment, and then her body flies to the side. Hard to tell if she's been hit or if she's jumped.

"That was you." Kim's voice returns as the picture swirls back into muddy water.

"And I died?"

"Not quite. Just your brain. You're hooked up to a machine. Want to see?" She speaks so matter-of-factly, she sounds creepy.

"Listen to you! Don't you have any feelings?"

Kim tilts her head again, looking confused. No wonder. It's what people always say to me, and I never understand why they're annoyed, either. You're supposed to feel sad when bad things happen, but you're not supposed to be a baby and cry about it. When my hamster died, I felt oddly guilty but announced it with a smile on my face, a nervous habit, and Mom freaked. Kim smiles that same way, too.

She seems so much like me. Maybe that's why we were such inseparable friends.

"Look." She points to the muddy water, and it swirls again. This time I can see into a hospital room. I can hear a machine *sish*, long in, and then *sish*, long out. A white sheet covers most of the body lying on that bed, but I can make out my head, all bandaged. My eyes are shut and swollen. One half of my face is purple and red.

It's my worst nightmare.

My mother sits beside me holding my hand. Her silver-thread hair is tied back loosely. Her thin pointy face looks pale against her shaggy, dark eyebrows. No one ever says "Like mother, like daughter" about us. "Paige, listen to me. You have to wake up. The doctor says you can't hear me, but I know different. Squeeze my hand if you can."

I squeeze my hand hard as I watch, but of course that body doesn't do anything.

"Wink hard, then, if you can't move your hand." My mother's voice sounds strong, nothing crybaby about her. But the skin around her eyes and mouth wrinkles into winces.

"Mom, I'm not in there anymore," I whisper. I reach out to touch her shoulder, and it feels as though I transported myself close beside her. Still, my hand passes through her.

"She can't hear you." Kim's voice comes from somewhere up above the hospital room.

I frown. Kim is right, of course, but I want to do something for Mom: kiss her cheek—I didn't do that a lot when I was alive—brush her loose strand of hair back, heck, throw her purse to the floor. Some gesture so she knows there is something bigger to my life than that shell of me *sishing* on that bed in front of her. "What's going to happen to me?" I turn toward Kim's voice and the image of the hospital room disappears. My consciousness comes back to the beach. "Am I going to lie in that bed forever or will the rest of me die, too?"

"Not unless your mom lets go. She needs to let them disconnect the respirator."

"And she won't?"

"Uh-uh."

"What about my dad?"

"She won't listen to him. He's too broken up to fight with her."

I shake my head. "I'll be stuck there forever."

"Then we'll play on the sand for a long, long time."

Anger boils up inside me till I want to claw at myself to release it. "I should have waited for Jasmine. None of this would have happened," I shout at the sky, which stays annoyingly perfect, bright blue, no clouds now.

"Maybe not," Kim says. She doesn't sound convinced.

"Definitely not! I never walk on the track! I should have stood up to those girls. They couldn't do anything worse to me than that train."

"You were mad at Jazz," Kim says.

"No, I wasn't!"

"Okay," Kim answers softly. She raises an eyebrow at me. One of the same almost nonexistent ones I grow over my eyes.

She's right, though. How could Jazz just dump me? And if I admit it to myself, it's worse than that. I felt so jealous of her. How could Jazz catch Cameron instead of me?

Kim pats at a sand wall, not looking up.

"I was afraid," I explain. "A coward. I hate those jock girls."

Kim starts shaping a pile of sand into a tower, ignoring me.

I stand up and kick at her castle. "I hate that I didn't help her. Hate," kick, "hate," kick, "hate" *myself* is what I don't say.

She gazes up at me, her eyes shining with tears.

I stop and kneel on the sand. "I'm sorry. I'll help you fix it."

"It's not the castle." She sniffs and wipes at her eyes. "You're just so angry. All the time."

"No, I'm not," I say flatly as I heap some mud from the hole into a pile. Inhaling deeply, I smell the fishy salt air. "Mostly, I force myself not to feel anything at all."

Overhead, a couple of seagulls shriek at each other. *Awk, awk, awk!* The waves *shh, shh* against the beach, and a fuzzy clump of bright green seaweed drifts in.

I stare at it. "Mom made kelp salad to keep us healthy."

"Food can't save you from a train. But all that healthy stuff will keep you alive in that bed."

"Great! That shell of me on the bed will shrivel up like old snakeskin." I rub hard at my eyes with the heels of my hands. When white spots float in front of me, I open them again. "I don't want to die yet! But I can't be that snakeskin, either. Living, somewhat breathing. Kimmee?" I wait till she turns and looks me in the eye. "Isn't there some way I can go back and fix this?"

"Press 'Edit, Undo'?" she asks.

I smile and nod. "Like we did when we made the comic strips on the computer?"

"Maybe," she says brightly. "I don't think you can stop from dying if that's your destiny, but I know some people have gone back a few days and changed some bits. I'd have to ask the older dead people."

"Could you? Tell them I need to help Jasmine. Then I'll be fine with all this."

She nods, stands up and walks into the water, fading with each step that she takes. When the waves lap at her shoulders, she totally disappears.

I collapse back on the sand and, just for something to do as I wait, dig at the hole Kim started. I'm dying in that hospital bed because I was a coward. If I can change even one half of that sentence, I will be happier. With the muck I scrape up, I form and shape a tower. At the top I make a turret, and by the time Kim's molecules form again over the ocean, I stick a seagull feather in the top.

Kim grins as she walks toward me.

"Good news?" I ask.

She nods, then points. "Nice flag." She kneels down beside me. "They like that you want to stand by your friend. So you get to go back. But only for seven days."

"Should be enough time to end things better."

"There's a couple of hitches." Kim seems to grow older in the way she speaks. More in command. "You can't let on, in any way, what will occur in the future. You can only use your knowledge from before the past week to make any changes."

I squint at her. "I don't really get that."

"You can't tell people you're going to die."

"Well, duh. Simple enough."

"Okay, but you can't yell at your mom for lying about me. 'Cause you don't know about me dying unless you dig up the information yourself."

"Right. I'll get on that one."

"You can be nicer to people, only not so nice that they think something's up."

"Nicer to people? All I want is to defend Jazz, not start some pay-it-forward campaign."

"Yes, but you can't tell Jazz that those girls are going to beat her up until you see it on that Facebook page."

"But they've always been like that. It's predictable."

She shrugs. "True. This is pretty tricky, which is why the elders hate letting people return. But if you do it wrong, you'll be back here even earlier."

"So the worst that could happen is . . . nothing," I suggest.

"Oh no. You could do real damage. You could bring others with you. Do you want to try or not?"

"What do I have to do? Close my eyes, click my heels, say a magic word?"

"No, just look down in the hole." She swirls the mud.

The Previous Monday Morning

∞

Hovering above, I watch myself opening my locker just as I did a week ago, first lunch break, pretending to concentrate on my locker combination. Suddenly, the way it often happens in a dream, I find myself inside that person actually spinning the dial around.

Down the hall, Vanessa argues loudly with Cameron, the same as she did the last time. No one pays that much attention. This is a drama that plays routinely. Sometimes Cameron yells, sometimes Vanessa cries. Usually, they break up. For a day or two at most.

"You were eyeballing that skirt. Don't lie!" Vanessa's eyes squint at him.

"Give it up, Van. You look at guys all the time," Cameron speaks in his reasonable voice. He stands squarely in front of her, his arms open wide, his palms spread out.

"Not . . . like . . . you." She jabs a pointed finger into

his chest with each word. "You give them the come-on."

"Like you don't." He's right, of course. They're both major players.

"Did you get that one's phone number?" she accuses.

He doesn't answer quickly enough, and Vanessa hauls back and swings at him. *Crack!* Like the sound of a whip.

Whoa! The noise still makes me jump.

All the kids in the hall freeze. No walking back and forth, no shuffling books. Everyone just stops to have a good stare at what comes next. Cameron's face turns soup red, but he doesn't lift a hand. This is different from their regular breakup routine. They always like to be front and center stage, but Vanessa never uses violence.

"Go ahead and call her, then. We're through." Vanessa flings her hair back over her shoulder and marches away.

Cameron stays frozen a few extra moments, shocked like everyone else around him. Then he wakes up. "Fine, I will," he answers loud enough for the spectators to hear. By that time Vanessa has already turned the corner.

Whose number does he have? I wondered last time. I even took my own cell out just in case. He may have asked someone for my number. Then I dashed to the cafeteria, ready to gossip with Jasmine about the lucky girl.

This time I walk with a sense of dread. I push through the double doors, the spicy smell of pizza hitting me as I slip into line and grab a tray. First break is crazy early to eat, yet we're all programmed to feel hungry then. I slide the tray along.

"How can you look at salad at ten in the morning?" Max says when I stop at the window with the bowls of spring mix behind it. He shakes his head in mock disgust. "Fresh and local in February, right?" There's an amused twist to his broad lips. On his tray sits a hamburger with orangey cheese drooling over the patty and bottom bun.

Last Monday I just rolled my eyes at him. But this time I figure nutrition and anticarcinogens don't need to be my main focus. Hamburger is the type of meat Mom most rails against—ground-up germs, she calls it. This is just a small payback to her for lying about Kim moving away. Besides, I want to taste meat at least once in my life. "You're right, Max. A mound of ground cow topped with saturated fat would be much better at this hour." I order one from the cafeteria lady.

"No fries?" she asks, a ladle of some in her hand already. "Comes with." She always looks disappointed when kids shake their head.

"What the heck. Sure, fries," I tell her.

She nods her hair-netted head in approval and beams as she dumps them beside my burger. She hands me the platter and I set it on my tray, sliding it along to the cashier. After I pay, I turn and look for a seat.

Max sits by himself at the nerd table. I put my tray there, too, waiting for Jazz.

That's when she runs in and almost knocks me over. "You'll never guess who I'm going to lunch with."

"Me," I suggest weakly. "Like always."

"Cameron!" She squeals and does a little shimmy. "Can you believe it?"

"Shhh!" I look around for Vanessa and her followers, something I didn't do last time.

Jazz ignores my warning. Instead, she throws her arms around me and forces me to shimmy with her. Her giddiness catches me up and I grin, too. "Great. Good for you."

"Do me a favor, Paige." She stops her shimmy. "Wait for me after school. Go help Mrs. Falkner till I come back."

"You're going with him after school, too?"

She nods, flashing a smile. "I'll tell you all about it later. You just need to walk home with me. My parents aren't from this century. You know that."

"Jazz, this isn't a good idea. Vanessa's really steamed at Cameron. Could you maybe wait till the body cools?" I watch her smile fade.

"What are you talking about? You know he'll just find someone else."

I frown. She's right. I can't argue further without telling her the future. Like she'd believe me, anyway.

"You know I'd do it for you," she says.

Of course, she won't have to. I will die first. In any case, my parents would let me hang out with Cameron. But unlike me, Jazz would willingly stand up for me, lie for me, protect me. I do get her point.

"Have fun," I finally tell her, and she gives me another hug.

"You're my best friend forever and ever," she tells me and leaves.

"I'll try to be," I answer under my breath.

"I don't know what you girls see in that guy," Max says, hamburger grease shining on his chin.

Last time that grease grossed me out. I looked away and ignored him the rest of lunch. This time I'm not going to let petty things force me into being more alone. Instead, I lean in and dab it away with my napkin. "Cameron's good-looking, what do you think?"

"So's Vanessa, but what about personality? They're like rattlesnakes."

"True." I shrug my shoulders. "But there's a certain excitement to a rattlesnake—the buzz, the anticipation." I close my eyes, inhale the meaty scent of my burger and bite in. Dense with texture and flavor, mmm. The juice runs down my chin now. How did my mother get so turned off by this?

"Nobody likes a nice guy," Max complains.

"Who's a nice guy? You?" I look directly at Max now. He has a broad nose and wide lips and wears his bangs squared across the top of his round face, not a looker for sure.

"Hey, I'm also funny, considerate. . . ."

"And short. Don't forget short." I sample the fries in between bites of burger. They're solid wedges of crispy potato.

"A lot of successful people are short. Movie stars, athletes . . . hey, I'm taller than you."

"No, you're not." This time around I don't feel as annoyed with Jazz or as deserted. Is it the fat in the food that is so soothing? Is it coming back from the dead that makes me more mellow? Or is it Max?

"Stand up." He grabs my arm and pulls me to my feet. "Right against me. Back to back." He turns and I feel his shoulders against mine, his body heat.

His hand pats down on the top of my head. "See, you're shorter."

"Honestly!" I turn. "You're standing on your tiptoes."

"Your sneakers have insoles."

I snort at that one.

"Will you be my friend?" he suddenly says.

"What?" I ask, squinting at him. Even from him, that sounds needy.

"I mean on Facebook."

"Oh. Ohhh! Sure. Why not?" I don't post a lot there, and Jazz is my only other real pal on the Net.

The bell rings then, and we head to science class.

Mr. Brewster hands out forms for our class trip to the science center this Thursday. "Body Worlds is a renowned exhibition, and we're very lucky to have this opportunity. We'll be seeing firsthand how the insides of our bodies look."

"Gross!" "Ew!" "Cool!" Vanessa's, Kierstead's and Max's reactions come at the same time.

I grin, silently agreeing with Max.

Next Mr. Brewster talks about cell division, something we're supposed to have read the night before. He dims the lights and shows us slides, especially focusing on mitosis. Fascinating stuff, but the room is warm and dark and I notice Abbi laying her head down on her arms.

Mr. Brewster notices, too. He strides toward her desk, and I see Kierstead lean over to warn Abbi. Too late. Mr. Brewster slams his ruler on her desk.

She startles awake, blinking the sleep from her eyes.

"Can you explain to the class what a genome is?" he asks her.

All she has to do is read off the slide. But, instead, she looks kind of fish-mouthed.

"Kierstead, can you help her out?"

Kierstead sweeps her long auburn hair back over her shoulder. "Who me, sir?" Silly delay tactic.

"Is there another Kierstead in the room?"

She bats her Bambi brown eyes and titters, hand over her mouth. Kierstead has been awake the whole time; how can she not know the answer? She looks over at Cameron, who winks. "I don't know. I guess I just don't get all this repro- duction stuff."

That gets a lot of laughs out of the whole class, not just the boys. Kierstead giggles along. It's the cool thing for girls to pretend they're stupid. Still, it's been so long since Kierstead has said anything intelligent, she doesn't really need to pretend anymore. Does she not even get what reproduction means?

"Paige, please enlighten Kierstead and Abbi."

I frown. Answering correctly will make me a target for them in the halls, at gym and at the overpass when the final showdown comes. I know this from the last time. All I have to do is pretend to be stupid, too, and they will leave me alone. The easy thing.

But stupid always makes me mad, and this is my final shot at life. "The genome is where the genetic information of the cell is stored." I point up to the slide. "It really says it all up there." Whoops, I shouldn't have added that bit. Worse than the previous time through when my description was more in depth.

"Way to go, smart girl!" Cameron winks at me.

Kierstead and Abbi put their fingers in *O*s around their eyes to make fun of my glasses, but I happen to know that Cameron thinks girls who wear them are hot. Especially when they take them off and show a whole new identity.

I remove my glasses for a minute and smile blurry-eyed at Cameron.

He blows me a kiss.

What am I thinking? This kind of thing is enough to get me hammered by Vanessa. That's if her underlings tell her about it.

But hasn't Kierstead been eyeballing Cameron, too? Flirting with him a little? If her phone number had been the one Cameron called, would she have turned him down to be loyal? I never really paid attention to her behavior last Monday. Now I store it for possible later use.

As the day wears on, through math, English and French, my stomach tightens, as though the hamburger and fries inside are doubling and tripling. They're also setting like cement so that I feel I'm lugging a boulder around. By dismissal, I just want to go home and flop across my bed, but I promised Jazz I'd wait for her. So, instead, I head to the library and ever so slowly shut off computers for Mrs. Falkner. When she looks busy somewhere else, I sit down, one arm pressing tightly against my middle to hold back the pain, and search the Net, typing in Kim's full name, Kimberly Ellis.

Kim said I can't confront my parents about her death unless I find the information about it myself. I stare at the screen. No one would dream that a waspy name like Kimberly Ellis belongs to a Chinese orphan, but of course she's become a "chosen daughter," as our parents preferred to call us. I don't even know her or my real names, for that matter.

An archived obituary notice comes up for the *Toronto Star*. Kim "succumbed to a sudden illness" in July seven years ago.

What is that illness?

I skim to the end of the column and see that her parents requested that, in lieu of flowers, donations be made to the Kidney Foundation of Canada.

What went wrong with Kim's kidneys? She was never sick, unless you count the time we both had chicken pox. And why wouldn't my parents let me go see Kim? Did she have something contagious? I know my mother is a germaphobe.

Was that why I hadn't been allowed to visit her? The obituary didn't give me any of these answers. For them I will need to confront Mom. Only, I have to do it carefully so as not to ruin the order of time and have my second chance end prematurely.

Monday after School

∞

"He's not what everyone thinks he is." Jazz's eyes shine as she bounces along the way home. "You think he's a big flirt, but he's really just friendly."

Jazz deludes herself. He's not just a big flirt, he's a major cheat. Still, "Uh-huh" is the only comment I can squeeze in.

"And he's sick of Vanessa. He's tired of her hissy fits." Jazz holds her shoulders back and her chin high. She smiles nonstop.

I pick my way across the icy walk more carefully. It's a gray, cold day, the same as it was the last time I lived through it, only today my belly holds a bucketful of greasy food. "Vanessa slapped Cameron. Did you know that? Do you understand that she is physically violent?"

Jazz is not hearing me. "Vanessa's a stupid cow," she says, and then, as if fate is striking her down, she slips and begins cartwheeling her arms to get her balance again.

I grab her hand to steady her. "Careful! Slow down." We head up the overpass now, me still holding on to her tightly. It isn't super high, which makes it a great place to train spot. If you stand there at the right time and the train comes toward you, the bridge shakes and it feels like you're going to be run right through.

My knees turn to jelly when I see the tracks. My arms shake and my teeth chatter. I can picture myself walking along one, can see the train approaching me, even hear the conductor sounding the horn. A short note, a longer note and then a longer, desperate, unending blast as it tosses my rag-doll body into the ditch. There's no way I can ever repeat stepping on a track again. If I am going to die the same way at the end of this week, someone will have to push me. I double over to ease the pain in my gut.

"You okay?" Jazz asks.

"Not really. I ate a hamburger today—it's killing me."

She shakes her head. "You never eat meat, and then you assault yourself like that?"

I nod. "It was great." I straighten. "Ow."

"There's no helping you." Jazz is vegetarian, and cows are sacred to serious Hindus. "You deserve what you get." She's kidding, but she's right. Just like being hit by a train when I bailed on my best friend, maybe I deserve to die for violating my parents' code of eating.

I try again to convince Jazz not to hang out with Cameron. "You say Cameron is just a friendly guy. But he was being very friendly to a lot of girls. And he was going out with Vanessa."

"Does she think she owns him?" Jazz asks.

"Uh-huh. That's exactly what she thinks."

"And you think I should back off because of her?"

At the top of the overpass, a blast of cold air stings my face. I nod. "Let him go out with other girls first. Abbi, and Kierstead, too. They all want him. Then they're the ones who stole him. Not you." Everything looks much closer than it is up here. I can see my house, storybook miniature in the distance, four long blocks away, the smoke curling up from the chimney invitingly.

Jazz turns to me. She's stopped smiling. "Did you know my mother wants me to go to India with her this summer?"

"Why do you look like that? Won't that be exciting?" I ask.

"Sure, I'm dying to go to India," she says sarcastically. "Just like you're dying to go to China." She starts walking again, more slowly.

Dying. I scrunch up my face. "That's different. I'll admit I have a mental block against a country that gave me up."

"Different, I'll say. You're still coming to my cousin Beena's engagement party this Saturday, right?"

"Yeah, but what's that got to do with you visiting India?"

"My aunt took Beena to India last summer. That's where she met Gurindar."

We start down the pass now, and I spot Dad's white truck

turning into our driveway. He usually leaves the house at four in the morning to get to the food terminal, so he often comes home early, too. All right, maybe I can ask him about Kim. He's way less emotional than Mom. I turn to Jazz. "Isn't it possible Beena just fell in love?"

"Yes. That's what everyone's saying: what a perfect love match it is. But it's only so perfect because he's a suitable Indian boy. Right down to his horoscope. Which is exactly what my parents want for me. And soon. Cameron might be my only chance to feel what real love is like."

"Aw, Jazz!" Is it real love, though? As the streetlights switch on against the dark of winter, I can see that even her skin glows. I don't want to stomp all over her happiness. Not this time through. For a moment, in fact, I want to hug her.

The moment passes, and it comes time for us to head down different streets. During the week, we never hang out. Homework, chores, maybe a bit of texting. School night is a sentence both sets of parents impose on us. But, nerds that we are, we don't really mind.

"So I'll see you tomorrow," Jazz says.

"Same time, same place." I give her a little wave. As she leaves, I double over again. Man, that hurts. Was it the burger or the fries?

Then I drag myself home the rest of the way. Inside I kick off my boots on my run up the stairs for the bathroom. I whip down my pants and sit on the toilet. *Relief!* I hate that Mom has to be right about a thing like a food group. But that's my parents' business: organic, healthy food.

When I'm done, I wash my hands and open the window wide. "Hello, Dad! I'm home!" I call as I head back down the stairs.

"Hi, Paige. Just unloading some groceries. Come and look at these beautiful mushrooms we got in today."

I head toward the kitchen. "Dad, what really happened to Kim?"

Dad turns from the counter to face me. He's a tall guy, kind of slow-moving, with long graying hair and large, calm horse eyes. But I see panic flicker briefly in them. "I'm fine. How was your day?"

"Terrible. You have no idea. My stomach is killing me."

"I'll make you some Rooibos." He fills the kettle and sets it to boil.

His shoulder blades move under his gray T-shirt, and I feel bad for a second. In a week, he won't ever perform this simple act of love for me again. "Okay. Really, Dad, was your day fine?"

He turns and smiles, lights twinkling back on in the brown of his eyes. "Well, there's these mushrooms." He dumps the bag on the counter.

The mushrooms are large and white. "Yeah, I can see how they would make your day."

"Besides that, I helped a guy buy the eggplant that was on his wife's grocery list." He hands me an oversize mug with antlers on it, a souvenir from our canoe week in Algonquin Park.

Sitting down at the counter and sipping the hot, sweet liquid, I feel soothed. Our kitchen is decorated, if you can even call it that, circa 1950. The cabinets are painted mint green; the counters are pale beige Formica; the floors are checkerboard tile. Jazz says it's like stepping into a malt shop from a classic television show.

"Dad, I was in the school library and thought I'd google Kim, just to see if I could friend her on Facebook."

He sips from his own tea, then releases a long sigh. "You found her death notice."

"Yeah. All this time, I thought she had left me without saying good-bye. It wasn't her fault."

"You're right."

"Why did you guys do that to me?"

"Paige." He says my name like an apology, then walks over to my stool and hugs me. "You were so young. We didn't know how to handle her illness or her death. Your mother fell to pieces."

"And I felt deserted."

"You would have felt the same way if you had watched her die. We all did. We loved Kim."

"Dad, what did she have? Was it contagious?" That would explain us not visiting her.

"No." He sips from his tea again and shakes his head. "An *E. coli* infection. They call it hamburger disease."

I sputter all my tea out.

"What's the matter with you?" He grabs a cloth and wipes up the tea.

"I ate a hamburger today."

"And you have a sore stomach?" He grabs the phone from the counter and keys in some numbers.

"Who are you calling? I'm okay now."

"The doctor. What are your symptoms?" Phone clutched to his ear, he touches my forehead. "Yes, hello?" He speaks into the receiver. "My daughter is suffering from food poisoning."

"Dad, really, I just had the runs."

"Diarrhea," he tells the person on the other end. "Any vomiting?" he asks me.

"No." I rub my stomach.

"You want us to wait twenty-four hours? Let me speak to the doctor."

"Honestly, my stomach doesn't hurt anymore," I say quietly, trying to calm him down.

"Fine! We'll go to Emergency." Dad slams the receiver down. "Come on, let's go!"

"I don't want to, Dad. Can we just wait, like they said?"

"By then it could be too late. Let's go."

I slide off my stool slowly. Trips to the hospital involve hours of waiting till someone sees you. I know that from my sprained ankle a couple of months ago.

Dad rushes for the door. "Put your boots on. Here," he says, grabbing our coats and throwing me mine.

Luckily, as we get to the car, Mom pulls up in the van.

"She ate a hamburger and feels sick," Dad calls to her as she climbs out. "We're going to the hospital."

"What! Why did you do that?" Her eyes open crazy wide. Sparks seem to fly from them.

"I wanted to try a burger just once before I died." *Whoops. Did I say that?* She doesn't seem to notice, anyway. "Mom, I don't need to go to Emergency. I have homework. Can we just stay home?"

She takes a breath, feels my forehead. "No fever." Her mouth crumples as she tries to decide.

"She had the runs," Dad tells her.

"Only once. I'll tell you if I feel sick again. You know waiting rooms are cesspools for germs." The last sentence is inspired, and it pushes her over the edge.

"Paige is right about that. Let's go back into the house, Tom, and wait."

My father's bottom lip buckles, but he nods. Mom leads the way, hanging her coat up in the hall closet and continuing into the kitchen. She slumps down at the table.

"Well, okay then. I guess I'll start supper." Dad begins getting stuff from the fridge, his usual cooking routine, only he slams the door and drops things.

I sit down beside Mom. "Dad told me about Kim."

Mom looks at me, her mouth dropping open.

"I saw her obituary on the Internet. Is that why we're vegetarians?"

After a moment, her mouth closes. "Yes," she finally answers. "We started Good Foods Market just after, too, so we could make sure people would have safe food."

I look back into her blue eyes, eyes that always remind me that she isn't my real mom. "When did she have the bad hamburger?"

Mom grabs my hand tightly. "You don't remember the last time you saw her?"

I shake my head.

"It was on your seventh Gotcha Day."

Cold fingers tingle down my spine. "I remember! We had a barbecue to celebrate." No one knows our exact birthdays so our parents celebrated the day they took us from the orphanage. Kim and I were adopted around the same time, so we celebrated together.

"She became sick immediately."

"From the burgers Dad cooked?" I grip her hand back.

"Mrs. Ellis bought them from a good butcher."

"But I didn't get sick."

"Maybe you didn't eat yours. You were always such a picky kid. Or maybe yours was cooked right through." Mom shrugs.

"People don't usually die from bad meat," Dad explains as he chops mushrooms at the counter. "Little kids, old people with—"

"Weakened immune systems," I finish for him.

"Right."

"Oh my gawd," I whisper. "It could have been me."

"We felt very lucky. Too lucky."

"So we didn't visit her."

"Your mom and I did, but she was so sick, she didn't know anybody," Dad says. "Hospitals aren't good places for young children. Your visiting would not have helped."

I pull my hand from Mom's. "It would have helped me."

"We didn't do the right thing, then. I'm sorry." Dad stares down at the mushrooms as if they were responsible. "We were just a mess."

"We intended to tell you. Someday. Once we got our own heads around it." Mom shrugs. "And then too much time passed."

It explains a lot.

"I'm sorry, too," she says softly.

"I get it." And I do understand, but somehow I still feel lied to and cheated.

"Seriously, is your stomach okay?" Dad asks. "Why don't we go to the walk-in clinic, just in case?"

"I'm fine." I try to smile but can't.

He hands Mom a cup of tea, giving me a sideways glance. Then he goes back to his chopping. I can smell onions frying and see a stack of white cubes piling up. Dad is making my favorite—tofu stroganoff. He puts a large pot of water on to boil for the egg noodles.

Mom asks me about my day as we wait for supper and try to act normal.

I tell her about Cameron and Vanessa breaking up. She only knows them vaguely from hearing about them and seeing them at school occasionally. But I tell her again how good-looking Cameron is and how all the girls like him. "Mom, he flirted with me, but he instantly made a move on Jasmine."

"You're all so young. Maybe he's attracted to both of you. He can't help that."

Dad begins serving supper. On Mom's plate, the stroganoff over the noodles looks creamy delicious.

He delivers my plate. On mine, the steaming rice is plain and white.

"Aw, come on, Dad. I haven't been to the bathroom since I came home. Can't I have some stroganoff?"

"Absolutely not. You have to rest your digestive system."

"You can have leftovers tomorrow for lunch," Mom says, touching my wrist.

"Great." I taste my rice. Bland as its color, as my life has been. "You know that Jazz can only spend lunch hours with Cameron? And I have to pretend she's volunteering at the library with me or she'll get in trouble with her folks."

"Don't they like Cameron?"

I swallow my dry rice. "They don't know him. It's just, he's a Westerner, and Jazz thinks they're shopping for a husband from India for her already."

"If Cameron is such a Casanova and goes along with her deceit, maybe he's not such a prize. Jasmine might be better off with a boyfriend her parents select."

Dad comes back on a statistic about divorces, and we have a discussion on romantic versus arranged marriages.

We had this same discussion last time, except, a few days later, there was a news story on Indian women who had been duped into marrying guys who were only after their dowries. Their families arranged those marriages.

After the revelation on Kim's death, it turns into a cozy evening, apart from the dry rice supper, and it's only afterward when I am on the computer looking up something for my history homework that I remember that Kim's parents had asked for donations to the Kidney Foundation. What does that have to do with *E. coli*?

Tuesday Morning

∞

Next morning Jazz knocks at our door, something that didn't happen last time. "Sorry I'm here early." She walks in, breathless. "I just couldn't stay at home a minute longer. My parents were talking about my grandmother finding a suitable boy for me."

"But they don't even know about Cameron." *How have I changed fate?* I wonder. The last time I lived through Monday, I didn't eat the stupid hamburger and fries, wasn't sick, ate a good supper. Oh man, then I got up, had cereal on my own and headed out early. I met her at her house, and we left right away. This morning, Mom insisted on taking my temperature, quizzing me on my bathroom episodes and serving me a digestion-friendly breakfast. "Why would your parents want a husband for you now?"

"I'm turning fifteen in February. They say I don't have to

get married right away. I can get engaged and still finish school."

"What about college? Can't you stall them at least? Tell them you need to concentrate on school."

"I'm not allowed to have an opinion at my house. They think I'm becoming rebellious. That's exactly why my uncle took my cousin Beena to India last year. I just had to get out of there, or I was going to blow it."

I frown, then point to the kitchen. "Want some breakfast? Granola with chia seeds? It will keep you regular." I raise my non-eyebrows at her.

"Is that what you had?"

"Nah. I had organic goat yogurt. I have to be gentle to my intestines. On account of my burger and fries yesterday."

Jazz chuckles at that one. "Thanks, I'm good. I ate a breakfast bar." It felt nice to distract her for a moment, but now her brow wrinkles. A dark ridge forms between her eyebrows.

"I'm sorry." I hesitate. "Do you want to talk to Mom or Dad about the India thing?"

"No. They can't do anything."

I shrug. "Maybe they can call Children's Aid."

"And Children's Aid will take me away from my family. How can I turn my back on them? Live with strangers. Oh!" She stops then and covers her mouth. "Sorry."

"No worries. It's different for me. I never knew my birth family."

"Didn't you ever want to find out about your real parents?" Jazz asks.

"Mom and Dad are real. They're enough. I don't need more." It's what our adoptive parents wanted us to think, we knew that instinctively, but of course both Kim and I always wondered, *Is my mom pretty? Is my dad strong?* We dug that hole to China all the time. Mom never liked it when we did.

"Let's just go." Jasmine hands me my coat from the closet.

I slip it on, step into my boots and grab my backpack. We walk side by side without saying anything for a while. I won't even try talking Jasmine out of seeing Cameron. Right now I have to agree that he is her last chance for real love. How sad is that?

"So you're going to visit your grandparents and cousins and aunts and uncles." I try to put a different spin on her trip away. "It must be great to know your whole family history like that."

We're nearing the schoolyard, the last block.

"You could try to trace your family, too, you know. I've heard your mom say anytime you want to go back to China, she would take you."

"Yeah, but . . ." I stop. Jazz's whole face begins to emit a glow. Her mouth stretches into a smile that almost reaches her ears.

From the blacktop, Cameron waves.

"You wave, too, in case anyone's watching," she says under her breath. "We're keeping us a secret till we're more sure."

In case Cameron wants to go back to the witch. I wave and grin just as broadly as Jasmine. A group of guys stand around Cameron. Are they bad-mouthing his ex, just the way the girls are Cameron?

We head straight in to our lockers.

At the other end of the hall, I notice a few of the second-string volleyball team—Gwyn, Emma and Zoe. They're talking in low voices. Gwyn looks our way and gives us a hard stare.

"Looks like your relationship's not that big a secret," I warn Jazz.

She smiles sweetly. "Hi, Gwyn. Heard you played a great game last Friday." M.M. Robinson won 34–28. Nothing unusual about that; they always win.

"Thanks," she sneers. How does Jazz know how Gwyn played? We weren't at the game.

The bell rings and I head to English class homeroom, which, my luck, I share with Emma, Gwyn and Vanessa. This is the day Mrs. Corbin decides to start our Shakespeare study for the year, and ironically the play she chooses is *Romeo and Juliet*.

She starts by showing us a list of famous quotations used in everyday life that come from the play. The line appears on the screen at the front with a page number, and she calls on various people to read out the passage the quote comes from.

The lines are interesting, but some of the kids stumble over the passages and that gets boring. Emma nudges me in the back and gives me a folded piece of paper. "Pass this to Vanessa," she whispers. "Don't look at it."

I turn around quickly. I don't want to pass their silly note. Why can't they just text each other like usual? But last class, Mrs. Corbin confiscated Emma's phone. Guess she learned her lesson. And because I didn't say no immediately, the paper now hangs between my thumb and forefinger. I listen as Gwyn reads the passage where Juliet asks about what is in a name and wince. Where was she back in grade four when we were taught about expressive reading?

Emma pokes me in the back, hard. "Ow," I call out.

"What's that note in your hand?" Mrs. Corbin asks.

"I . . . I don't know," I answer, dropping it to the desk like it's on fire. I sound like all those other stupid girls and hate myself for it.

"Open it up and read it to the class, then," Mrs. Corbin says.

I scrunch up my mouth and unfold the paper, once, twice and three times, slowly, delaying to try to think of some way out of this. It's too big a paper to chew and swallow. I curse Emma in the long moments, as nothing comes to me. I read the note to myself first.

Vanessa,

Can you believe it? Cameron's going out with Banana. We saw him make goo-goo eyes at her this morning.

Emma

What! They think I'm going out with Cameron! Of

course, it makes sense since he winked and blew a kiss at me in class yesterday. And we waved at each other this morning. Hadn't I hoped I was the one he was calling on Monday?

"We're waiting, Paige," Mrs. Corbin says, arms folded across her chest.

"It's not appropriate to read out loud," I say in desperation.

But it works.

"Very well. You may throw it in the wastepaper basket. Since you all like writing notes so much, you'll be happy to know your assignment is to read the first act of *Romeo and Juliet* and summarize it in one page. It is to be turned in tomorrow. You can start on that now."

There are groans, but I feel my skin cool to its normal temperature. A temporary reprieve. Vanessa will find out between the next classes about me being Cameron's supposed chosen one.

I'll be the one the volleyball team will want to beat up.

"Way to go, Banana," Emma says as she jabs me in the back again, hard.

I bite down on my tongue so as not to cry out. This will be a different way to stand up for Jazz. I will stand in for her instead.

We read till the end of the period. Why do Romeo and Juliet fall for each other, anyway? And how so quickly and deeply? Why can't they just settle for a nice cousin their parents choose for them?

Poor Jasmine. I rush out when the period ends and catch up with her on our way to math. "They think I'm going out with Cameron," I whisper.

"Seriously?" She sounds too shocked.

I feel like pinching her.

But she hugs me instead. "This is great. He can play along with that, and we'll make sure my parents never know."

"It's perfect, all right." I hug her back. This is why I'm here, after all, to stand up for her against these bullies. If I'm the victim, fine. It's a way better reason to go into a coma. But another thought occurs to me. Only some events from before are re-occurring and some new things are happening. An altered destiny. Is it possible to alter destiny just a little more?

At lunchtime I leave my thermos of stroganoff in the locker and suggest to Max that we eat at the mall with Cameron and Jazz.

"Sure. We can have the three-side special at Wong's."

"I hate Chinese," I say, but then reconsider. "Does it have any monosodium glutamate in it?"

"Oh plenty. Makes it taste good." He grins.

"All right, then." Everyone knows food-court Chinese isn't authentic, not like they serve dog or cat or even shark-fin soup. It resembles real Chinese about as much as Mickey Mouse does a real rodent. There is no reason to avoid it. We stroll off the school grounds, my arm linked through Cameron's. I have to admit, that feels good. He is definitely taller than both Jazz and me, and he has broad shoulders and muscled athlete's arms.

Max walks on Cameron's side and Jasmine on mine. If her mother drives by right now, she might even call my mother to warn her about me going out with Cameron. Jasmine and Max look like they're just chumming along. But no parents see us. Only the volleyball team.

I notice them huddled at the far end of the football field on the other side of the fence, watching us and puffing. Not from the cold, either. I can't believe a bunch of jocks would do that to their bodies. They're smoking.

I lean into Cameron just to make it look really good, and we keep walking.

In the mall, too, we continue along with Cameron and me attached to each other. I realize this playacting is my last chance at any kind of romance, too. But when we sit down at a table in the food court, boys across from girls, Jazz and Cameron don't have to touch. The energy between them hums and pulses, a growing live thing. Our playacting has nothing to do with love.

They share a plate of bo-bo balls, and Max helps me order my sides. I discover spareribs in garlic honey sauce aren't half bad. Too bad a pig has to die for them. The fried rice and the Cantonese chow mein are delicious. Little bits of animal flesh in that, too. This can't be the way my bio parents eat. Dad once told me they were poor, starving even, and they definitely couldn't afford meat.

Kim is right about a lot of things. I was so angry before and never realized it. This time through, it's as if my fists are unclenching. And when I stop feeling so much hatred toward my bio parents, I begin to feel curious.

Pretending to be Cameron's girlfriend feels pretty good, too, better than being linked to Max, the school geek. That is, until gym class.

Because of a presentation in the gym, the volleyball nets have been taken down. They need to be set up again. Mrs. Brown sends a couple of the girls from the volleyball team to get the poles and me and Zoe for the net. I should be safe with the teacher watching.

But as Rebecca and Gwyn join to lift the first pole from the storage room, I can't get out of their way fast enough. They back out and "accidentally" swing it so hard that I trip over it, face-planting on the laminate floor.

"Oh no! Sorry! Paige, are you all right!" Emma sounds like she really means it.

Gwyn actually cries. The class gathers round in a concerned circle. No one but Mrs. Brown is fooled. The message is clear: *Mess with Van and your legs get smashed.*

Mrs. Brown feels along my left shinbone, then my right. "Where does it hurt?" she asks.

"I don't feel anything," I answer, but I can see the welt across the front of my legs deepen in color.

"We should call your parents," Mrs. Brown says.

"No, no!" They will take me to Emergency; they will

fuss. I'll miss days of my life at home with my legs up.

"Let's see if you can stand, then."

I refuse Emma's hand and gather myself up slowly. If I keep my weight on my heels, I'll be fine.

"Gwyn, go get some ice from the office," Mrs. Brown commands.

I sit out the rest of the period on the bench, legs stretched in front of me with ice packs on my shins. I count myself lucky. If I hadn't tripped, I might have been in double casts.

Tuesday Afternoon

∞

B y the end of the day, my legs throb and I can't walk at a normal pace. All chance of hiding the incident from Jazz fails. "They bashed me with the volleyball poles," I tell her as I limp off the school grounds with her.

Jazz nods. "Rebecca passed me a note in history. It said I better tell my friend Banana to keep her hands off what doesn't belong to her. Or more than just her legs will hurt." Jazz throws her arms around me and hugs desperately. "I'm sorry. I never thought they would do anything like this."

"I did." I shrug. "Some bruises, not a big deal. This guy means something to you, right?" Over Jazz's shoulders I suddenly spot Vanessa heading for a low, black sports car parked on the street.

A woman with bright red hair stands near it, smoking.

Her jeans are a slim fit, and she wears thigh-high black boots with laces and a poofy white sleeveless jacket over a red sweater. The tires on the car look as fat as her lips. Her eyes squint hard against the smoke from the cigarette, the hardness a family trait. She has to be Vanessa's mother.

Wow. Imagine having a mom who actually fits and looks at home in the boutique styles. Mine wears jean dresses designed to hide her body, and her silver hair always parts in the middle no matter what kind of style the salon tries on her— my adoptive mom, anyway. Who knows what my real mother wears.

As Vanessa draws closer, her mother grabs her by the shoulders and shakes her, carping at her all the while about taking cigarettes from her purse. Vanessa must answer her back, and the woman winds up and slaps her.

Vanessa's face sets into stone, even as a hand mark reddens on her cheek. The woman shoves her toward the car, and Vanessa scrambles in. The driver's door slams and bright orange sparks hit the road as the car pulls away.

Maybe there are advantages to not looking like your mother. No one ever guesses Mom and I are related. Mom's pink skin sunburns too easily, and beneath her jet black eyebrows, her faded blue eyes are rounder than my brown ones. But when Mom looks at me, her eyes are as gentle as her voice, even when she's tired or annoyed. I wonder if my birth mother could be as patient. Would poverty make her as mean as Vanessa's mom?

In a split second, a window has opened to Vanessa's life away from school. Something in that view tells me she needs Cameron just as much as Jazz.

"He's never going to go out with her again," Jazz tells me, as though she knows what I'm thinking. "He's told me that over and over. Whether my parents send me to India or those girls toss me into a ditch, Vanessa will not get him back."

Toss her in the ditch, I hope not. "Maybe you're right," I say. Something suddenly becomes as clear to me as that split-second window into Vanessa's life. "For her, it's not about getting him back, it's about getting even."

When we arrive at our usual intersection, Jazz offers to walk me all the way to my doorstep, but I tell her it isn't necessary. I limp home, grateful to have at least this pain that proves my loyalty to her.

Nobody is at the house when I step in, and that aloneness decides it for me. I want to find out more about my birth family, and Mom doesn't ever have to know. I don't even take off my boots or coat, just hobble up the stairs, clutching the banister. I know where she keeps important documents. A metal box sits at the bottom of her walk-in closet in the bedroom. It has a latch on it but no lock. Their lives are contained in an open but flameproof box.

Any time I want, Mom will take me to China to get in contact with my roots—hasn't she said that a million times? So why do I rush for that box in the closet, limping as fast as I can? Is it so that I can look in it before I change my mind? All the hundreds of opportunities I had to search it before, I never bothered. Afraid of what I might find out. Or do I hurry so I won't get caught by my mother?

Both, I decide. I flick on the light and kneel down at the back among all the shoes, keeping the door open so I can hear if someone comes in. My mom keeps things in file folders, and I flip through them till I hit one that says "He Fuyi."

A Chinese name. My Chinese name? I quickly pull it out.

Inside is a stack of papers. Of course, I never went to those Mandarin lessons Mom offered to send me to, so the characters don't mean anything to me. The top paper appears to be a copy of a newspaper clipping from what looks like a classified section.

Across it is a row of baby pictures, each with a column of notes underneath it in Chinese script. All babies look alike to me, and in this strip the younger infants appear round-cheeked with closed, puffy eyes and nearly bald heads. Straggly black bangs, tiny noses, upside-down half-moon mouths, the toddler faces also have a lot in common. Their eyes seem to question, maybe even implore. How did my mom choose the little girl with no eyebrows? She'd circled my photo. Underneath the row, someone had jotted notes:

Finding Ad in the local newspaper. He Fuyi was found abandoned under the lamppost at the back door of the nursery of Hechuan SWI. She is in good health, nothing left on her when she was found.

So He Fuyi has to be my name. Two babies to the right of me, another toddler is circled, same eyes and bangs; she doesn't have any eyebrows to speak of, either, but her mouth opens into an *O*. One word is scrawled beneath her: *Kim*. It's Mom's handwriting. I didn't know we'd been adopted from the same orphanage. We may even have played together back in China. If only she had lived, we could still have been friends. To have someone who had been through all the same experiences as I had might have made me a different person.

There is a Certificate of Adoption, listing my parents' names as adoptive parents and a date: July 14. My Gotcha Day, the closest thing to a birthday that I can celebrate. The next paper is a Children's Medical Examination Record, but while the questions are listed in both languages, the answers are only in Chinese script, each character a little picture. I thumb through the pages and come to the final document. The header on this one squeezes at my heart: Certificate of Abandonment.

I skim the information, which is basically the same as on the newspaper copy. The last sentence stays with me. "We have tried hard but can't locate her natural parents up to now. This is to certify that she is an abandoned baby." Underneath in bold are the words Chongqing Hechuan District Social Welfare Institute and a date.

How many people can say they have been officially abandoned?

My throat tightens and I squeeze my eyes closed. I hear a noise. What is that? No time to cry about any of this. I shove the papers back in the file folder and slip it back into the metal box, slamming the lid.

I run out of my parents' bedroom but know I won't make it down the stairs in time.

"Paige?" My mother stands on the landing. "What are you doing up here in your coat and boots?"

"Just had to go to the bathroom, Mom," I answer.

"In such a big hurry?" She touches my forehead. "Do you still have diarrhea? Your dad was right. We should have gone to the hospital."

"Relax. I drank a lot of water after gym class today."

"But you look so . . . upset." Mom stares at me intently. "Is something else going on?"

"No, nothing, I swear." I meet her eyes. "Going down to do my homework now."

"All right. I brought home some yogurt-covered raisins for you."

"Thanks." I wait till she turns away to start down the stairs. I don't want her to notice my limp. At the bottom, I hang up my coat and set my boots carefully on the tray beneath it. Then I go to the den and sit at the computer. He Fuyi, my real name. I might have been a different person had I grown up with it. What does it even mean?

I open the Internet browser and type my Chinese name in, hoping for some glimpse of a family that could be mine. "He" had to be my surname and "Fuyi" my given name. But searching by "He" produces hits that refer to "He" as in the pronoun. Searching under "Fuyi" produces some Chinese restaurants and other sites in script. When I use the whole name, I find sites that mention "He" as a pronoun right beside some guy's first name, "Fuyi." I give up in frustration and go to Facebook just to relax.

There is Max's friendship request. I click "Confirm," then "Message," where I type, Hey, Max, do you know any Chinese?

By that time, Mom calls me. "Paige, I could use your help with supper!"

"Just a minute."

Max's answer comes up quickly. He must have been on the computer. *Nerd.* I smile. Nerds are people I understand.

Max Liu: I know some Mandarin. Parents made me take lessons.

I type in, Do you know what the name Fuyi means?

"Paige, I need these yams chopped now. Or supper won't be done for hours," Mom calls.

"Coming."

Max Liu: Fu means luck or fortune. Yi could mean a lot of things. Do you have the Chinese symbols for Yi? My father could tell you.

His dad is probably so Chinese he pronounces his *R*s as *W*s. Even so, I am jealous. I type back. I'll bring them to you tomorrow. Gotta go.

I head straight to the counter and start on the orange potatoes.

"How was school today?" Mom asks in a stiff voice. Her back is to me as she stirs some onions in a frying pan.

"Fine. Can you sign my permissions note for the trip to the science center? And do you have thirty dollars to pay for it?" I chop at the large hard yam. Just once couldn't we have plain white potatoes?

"Why do you need my thirty dollars? Don't you have plenty of money yourself?"

I squint at her. "You want me to pay for a field trip out of my allowance?"

"No. I want you to pay with the money you took from me." She turns from the stove to face me. "I kept a hundred-dollar bill in my jewelry box and now it's gone." She jabs a finger toward me. "You left tracks to my bedroom."

"What? I didn't take any money."

"Then why are you acting so strange?" Her voice cracks. She sounds as if she's about to cry. "Are you on drugs, Paige?" She grabs my face and stares into my eyes.

"Stop! Of course not." Abusing your body like that would be the supreme sin in our house. "Mom, there's stuff going on in my life, yes. Nothing like that, though."

"Then what happened to the hundred-dollar bill?"

"I dunno. Did it fall down into your underwear drawer?"

"You can talk to me about anything, you know that, Paige."

I get hit by a train on Monday after school, and then I'll be in a coma forever because you won't let me die. "No, Mom. I can't talk to you about everything. You like to think I can, but I can't."

So Mom ends up not talking to me, which isn't that bad. I don't want to explain my tracks to her bedroom. In fact, I want to sneak back into her closet storage box and retrieve something with my name in Chinese script. When Dad calls to say he's at the mechanic's with the truck—it needs a new alternator—he provides the perfect distraction. Mom drives over to pick him up.

I head back to that metal box and pull the folder on He Fuyi. I look through the papers and remove the Certificate of Abandonment. There are three Chinese scripts below my name. My real name. Three scripts that might be code for something important about me.

I fold up the certificate and tuck it into my jeans pocket. Then I shut the box and straighten the shoes in the back of the closet. I squint at the floor. It's a varnished oak that Mom is pretty proud of. In a certain light, will my footprints show? Washing the wood might look suspicious. I grab a bath towel and swish it awkwardly with my foot, then I head back out and toss the towel in my hamper. That done, I sit in my room, reading *Romeo and Juliet* and making notes.

The door bangs open downstairs. "Paige!" my mother bellows, her silent treatment obviously over.

"Up here," I say in a normal tone, hoping to delay her invasion by another moment.

Mom arrives at the door of my room, breathless. "Paige! I'm so sorry. You didn't take the money, after all."

"Duh! I know that."

"I should have known, too. I'm sorry. It's just you had such a guilty expression on your face. And you looked like you'd been crying."

I don't answer her.

"Anyhow. Your father took the bill from my jewelry box." She points behind her shoulder with her thumb to where Dad now stands, looking sheepish. "He needed money for the truck and thought the credit card might be maxed out." She stops to hug me. "It wasn't the money, Paige. I was just so worried you were into drugs."

The warmth of her arms around me, her worry, her guilt, I enjoy it all for a moment. Then I shrug away. Being abandoned, officially, has a strange effect on me. I should be hurt and angry with my bio family, but for some reason I'm upset with Mom. All that love and attention that I want to come from a different person or family. "Um, can you sign the form for the science center now? And give me thirty dollars?"

Mom looks at Dad and then back at me. She wants to say something else. "Of course, dear. Do you have a pen?" She takes two twenties and a ten out. "Keep the extra money to buy lunch or a souvenir." A second apology. "I love you very much." A third.

"I know, Mom." I should tell her I love her back. "Thanks." But I can't because I really don't feel anything at that moment.

We eat a late supper of Moroccan stew. I take a second helping to prove, once again, that my stomach is fine and that I'm not taking drugs.

Dad talks about the truck. Mom tells us about what the food network says about blueberry juice. I mention how I went out to lunch with Jazz, Cameron and Max.

"Nothing fried, I hope," Dad said.

"Chinese food," I answer evasively. "That's mostly healthy, isn't it?"

"Chinese? I thought you hated anything to do with your homeland. Of course, some of it's healthy. We trust you to make the right choices."

Not always. I don't throw Mom's earlier mistake back in her face. We can talk about everything, Mom says, but that's only true as long as everything is just nothing.

Wednesday Morning

∞

Next morning, the air warms just enough to turn the dampness into a thick fog. It's like walking through wet cotton to get to school. The icy moisture seeps under my jacket, and I shrug my shoulders against it. I meet Jasmine at our usual corner, bumping into her before seeing her. "Hey, Jazz. Guess what? I found out what my Chinese name is."

"Yeah, what?" She hunches her own shoulders and shivers.

"He Fuyi," I answer. "My last name is He."

"Great. So now you can find your real parents," she says.

"My real parents are right here!" I snap, a knee-jerk reaction. But isn't it what Kim and I used to dig in the sand for all the time? To reach China and find our other more "real" parents?

"You know what I mean," Jazz says. "Maybe you're related to some emperor and got swapped at birth."

"It's a possibility." I pause. "Not." Wealthy, titled parents are no longer in my faintest expectations. What I most want from my biological parents now is to know they feel regret. That if and when they see me, they will be astounded at how smart and beautiful I am and how well I am doing. And realize they should never have given me up. "What if they have no teeth, are cross-eyed and want money from me?"

"Then you'll run like crazy and never make contact again. It's not like you owe them something."

"They abandoned me. I don't owe them anything," I repeat.

"Just what I said." Jazz stretches an arm out in front of her. "Geez, I can't see my hand in front of my face. Are we almost at school?"

"I think we passed it," I answer. "At least, I hope we did."

"Did I tell you my mom wants me to start helping in the kitchen?"

"Gawd, you do so much already."

"She wants me to learn the Punjabi staples." She puts on her Indian accent. "Every good wife must know how to make *paratha*."

"Uh-oh. How does Cameron feel about Indian food?" I ask.

"He loves it." Jazz gets that dreamy look on her face.

"Can't he convert or something, then?" I ask.

Jazz chuckles. "To Indian food?"

"No, to the culture. How can he become suitable to your parents?"

"For a starter, he'd have to commit to marriage. Not like either of us wants that yet."

"Neither of you wants that. You'll have to make that plain to your mom. Stop! Wait!" I grab Jazz's arm. Out there in the fog, there's something or somebody. Suddenly, a large body jumps out at us.

"Ah!" I shriek.

"Just me!" Cameron smiles and bends down to kiss Jasmine's face.

My heart thumps back to its normal rate again.

Meanwhile, the kiss lasts too long. Embarrassing. There's nowhere else to look.

"Paige!" another voice calls from directly behind us. *Max! Great.* It's a relief to be rescued.

"Do you want to come to my parents' restaurant first break?" He joins me, and we continue walking while Jasmine and Cameron kiss.

He's asking me out for lunch. I panic. Max is way more fun than I expected. Still, lunch. "I can't eat Chinese two days in a row."

"What are you talking about? You want your name translated."

I'm wrong. "Oh yeah, I just meant . . . well, you know . . . sure, first break would be good."

"Listen, then. Keep your coat with you and bring your afternoon books along. Save time. We'll probably be late as it is."

The fog doesn't lift by the time we reach the school. But that black sports car pulls up in the bus zone, and Vanessa jumps out. Has she spotted Jazz with Cameron? They're walking behind me and Max, so I can't see whether they're hand in hand or cuddling. Or maybe even kissing.

I can't tell from Vanessa's face, either. It never registers anything. She brushes past us and heads for the far edge of the football field.

In first class, English, we're back to *Romeo and Juliet*, which isn't a new play to me. My parents took me and Jazz to see it in High Park last summer. Besides, doesn't everyone know it doesn't end well for the star-crossed lovers? Still, I remember watching the story unfold, and now it's the same reading it. I can't help hoping that, this time, Juliet's parents will come around. This time Romeo will understand she's only faking death. This time he won't kill himself, and then Juliet won't wake up and have to commit suicide herself.

I guess that's how I feel about my date with the train on Monday, too. Why listen and study and make notes if I don't think the outcome can be different?

First break comes and Max grabs my hand. I don't even pull it away. "We have to hurry. Dad said he'd have lunch ready."

I don't tell him again that I don't want to eat Chinese. I just rush along beside him, happy to get away from school and the volleyball team.

We hop a bus to the downtown core and get off at the lake. There's a Vietnamese takeout on one side and a sushi bar across the street. Next to it is an upscale pizza restaurant. That's the one Max takes me to. Big shock. We walk through the door.

"Hi, Max. And you must be Paige." A tall smiling man holds out his hand to me and I shake it.

"Hi." I'm blown away. No Chinese accent, and Max's dad is handsome. His blue-black hair is swept to one side, and he sports a nicely manicured beard. He wears a burgundy-colored apron over a matching shirt with a round collar.

"Your pizza is cooling over at the table by the window." He walks with us to our seats. "Do you have the script?"

I hand him my Certificate of Abandonment, and he immediately begins studying it. Meanwhile, I check out the view of the park and lake across the street. Choppy gray waves stretch all the way to Hamilton. A lone dog walker guides four black Labs along the seawall.

"Better eat right away or you'll be late," his dad says, not looking up.

I turn my attention to the pizza, pick up a slice and bite in. Mmm. Bacon and eggs with some kind of cheese on a thin crust. Good to experience bacon before I die.

"It's interesting," Mr. Liu says, stroking his beard, "that your parents even gave you a name."

"Do you think they maybe wanted me to look for them?" I ask.

Mr. Liu tilts his head and purses his lips. Seems like an unspoken no. "I think they wanted you to have a better life than they could offer."

"They wanted to have a boy instead of a girl, so they had to dump me," I grumble.

He shakes his head. "You know they used to kill baby girls. Boys got them land, girls just cost them dowries."

"Being adopted is a way better deal," Max says.

"So you don't think I should head to China to find them?" I ask his father.

"There are more than a billion people in China. Probably a million or so have your surname."

Again that seems like a no, which is a relief, in a way. If I can't change fate, there isn't enough time to get a passport, let alone fly to China, and to tell the truth, I still balk at the idea of visiting a country that hates girls so much.

"Was I right about 'fortune'? Does her name have something to do with good luck?"

"Fortune in the arts," his father says. "Are you artistically inclined, by any chance?"

"No." My heart sinks. I'm not the person my parents thought I would be. "I'm more your cliché Chinese girl, interested in the sciences." I try to smile.

"Paige is a nice name," Max suggests brightly.

"For a writer," I answer.

"What's in a name?" Mr. Liu says, shrugging his shoulders.

"*Romeo and Juliet*," I say.

"Act two, scene two," Max adds.

Max's dad smiles broadly. "Do I look like a Victor? That's my first name."

He does look like a winner, although the name has an old-fashioned ring to it. I shrug. "Thanks for translating." I wave the slice I'm eating. "And the pizza."

"No problem. Nice to meet you." He has to excuse himself to help out in the kitchen.

Afterward, I watch Max differently as he wipes his chin. His wide nose, lips and the shape of his jawline resemble his dad's, and you can see that when he grows taller and styles his hair, he will be handsome, too. It would be very interesting to be his friend, grow up alongside him and watch the transformation. Only I'm pretty sure I won't be around to see it.

Wednesday Afternoon

∞

We step off the bus in front of the school just as the bell rings. At least one team member should spot us from a classroom window. By now the volleyball team must know that I'm not Cameron's chosen one. Me hanging with Max should be a big clue. But that doesn't mean they let up on me. By the time I walk into French class on the third floor, I must be a total of five minutes late.

Madame Potvin chooses not to notice, but Kierstead speaks up to point it out. "Shouldn't Paige get a late slip?"

"*En français, s'il vous plaît,*" Madame P answers.

Kierstead rolls her big brown eyes. She opens her pouty mouth and tries, "*Est-ce que* Paige . . . ," then huffs in frustration. "Oh, never mind."

I smile. The joy of acting stupid to be cool. Kierstead doesn't come off too great today.

Madame Potvin looks directly at me. "*Pas encore*, Paige." My warning.

"*D'accord*," I agree. "*Je m'excuse*." Being late isn't a habit of mine, anyway.

"Teacher's pet," Kierstead grumbles.

I shrug. I like learning a new language and speaking French. The grammar rules seem way more logical than in English. More logical than people, too. Let's face it, Kierstead is trying to get even with me over the Cameron/Vanessa breakup, when she is just itching to go out with Cameron herself.

Later Madame P wants someone to conjugate the verb *être* with *en retard*, so she calls on me, her idea of showing the class that she hasn't entirely let me off the hook for slipping in after the bell. *I am late, you are late* (singular informal), *he/she is late, you are late* (plural formal), *we are late, they are late*, I rhyme them all off perfectly in French.

Better late than dead, I think to myself ruefully. If I'd left later on Monday, I would still be alive and living through next week instead of trying to improve on this last one.

Next break, Morgan and Laura march toward me in the hall, only parting slightly to knock me hard from either side.

"Ow!" I squawk.

"Excuse us," Laura calls.

"You all right?" Max rushes to me. He's sweet. Last time they bulldozed me, too, but no one was around to sympathize. No Max, and Jazz was busy with Cameron. "What's with them, anyway?"

"Dunno. They might think I'm going out with Cameron." Although last time they knocked me, it was just because I was friends with the person going out with him.

"Well, that's ridiculous." Max slips his arm around me. "You're going out with me," he says loudly.

Okay, well this is a predicament. Being his friend is more fun than I thought. It's a little embarrassing to have this short boy's arm around my waist, though. I can feel my skin turn red. *Or is that orange*, I wonder, *when you add pink to yellow?*

He kisses my cheek.

I squawk again.

"Too much?" he asks. He speaks softly, "I just thought it would make them leave you alone."

"Uh-huh."

"Anyhow, it felt nice," he adds.

Strangely, it did. My cheek still tingles, but I find I can't admit this so I just punch his shoulder and grin.

He takes my hand and walks me to science class. It feels weird, but I don't shake him off. "Sit with me on the bus tomorrow?" Max asks before we go in.

"What? Oh, you mean for the trip to Body Worlds!"

Max smiles, taking the return of my memory as a yes. "It's going to be great. My doctor said it was the finest form of mummification. The organs are really well preserved."

I so looked forward to that, last time. But sitting alone on the bus, with the big space beside me advertising *loser*, hadn't been that much fun. Wandering the exhibit alone hadn't been great, either. Abbi tripped me and after, as I lay sprawled on the floor, Kierstead stepped on my legs. Mr. Brewster saw what happened and lectured them about running in the museum.

They apologized—what could I say to their mumbled-under-the-breath "sorry"? "Whatever"—then they snickered into their hands when Mr. Brewster headed to another exhibit.

Will it be better walking around with Max? Are you any more of a nerd if you group yourself with another brainiac? Stupid haircut, hooded brown eyes, short, a bit squat even, a nice guy destined to become good-looking. His smile isn't dazzling, but it's pleasant. This time around I want company and, if I can admit it to myself, Max's company. I don't care what anyone thinks.

"Yeah, let's sit together, Max."

At the end of the day, I don't know whether his hand-holding thing works at all because someone took a marker to my locker. *Browner. Geek. Banana. Ho.*

And my personal favorite: *You're dead!*

By the time Jazz finally returns from her mall wanderings with Cameron, I've borrowed some paint remover from one of the cleaning ladies. The letters are barely visible.

"I had such a great time!" Jazz hugs me. "Thank you for covering. We've finally decided to make it official and go public."

"But what about your parents?" I ask.

"Never! Public at school, not at home." She tucks her arm in mine and we head out of the building.

"I don't know if that's such a good idea."

This Wednesday's weather seems different than last Wednesday's, though. Drearier? The air still feels as cold and damp as it did this morning, but the fog has cleared. The gray snow slops against my feet. I can feel the wet seeping in. "I mean, I've already had the leg bashing. Do you want that?"

"Cameron will protect me." She smiles, all moony.

"Well, then, he's got to start walking you home, Jazz." I don't look at her to see if she's still smiling.

"But for that I have you."

I sigh. "I'll do my best." It all feels so hopeless to me. I can't change how Jazz feels about anything. Can't talk her into not going out with him. Can't even make her hide it anymore. The only thing I can do is stand alongside her against ten girls on Monday. It's like watching *Romeo and Juliet* again.

So I change the subject. "What Punjabi specialty do you have to learn tonight?"

"Oh, don't get me started!" Jazz complains. But apparently I already have. The rest of the way, she talks about making bread from scratch, *roti* and *naan*, *chapati*, *paratha* . . . so many. "They're shoving their way of life down my throat. I mean, who needs that many carbs!"

The rest of the way, she also manages to make me

envious that she knows her background and culture. That she lives with her "real" family. When I leave her, I decide I will talk to my mother. If anyone knows how to track down my biological family, she's the one. After all, isn't she the parent stubbornly holding the hand of my comatose body on some other plane of existence?

I say good-bye to Jasmine and hurry home.

Usually my parents take turns spelling each other off at the store, Dad coming home always around four. 'Course that day both are late, so I defrost some eggplant balls and start some pasta.

When Mom comes in, she comments on how good it smells and hugs me. I try to hug back and then launch into The Conversation.

"Jasmine is talking a lot about her trip to India. She's worried about the marriage thing, of course. But she got me thinking. She has grandparents, aunts and uncles and even cousins there."

Mom heads me off. "You have cousins and aunts and uncles, right here."

"Yes, but they're not blood related. I don't have any real family history. Kim is about as close as I got."

Mom stares at me, fish-mouthed for a moment. Then she speaks. "Okay, we can book our trip to China this summer. I've always planned for us to go. We can see the Great Wall, Tiananmen Square. . . ."

"Those are landmarks, not family."

Mom chews at her lip. "That's true. But you can get to know your culture, the history of your people, the language. You can feel closer to your roots that way."

"Mom, I don't want culture. I don't want to go to China, either. Can't we look for my real family? E-mail the orphanage for records?"

Mom smiles. "Honey, we don't even have so much as a scrap of clothing left from your biological family. We don't even know your name."

"Oh yeah?" I produce the folded-up Certificate of Abandonment from my pocket. "Isn't my Chinese name He Fuyi?"

"So you *were* in my bedroom yesterday." Mom frowns and shakes her head. Her pale skin turns pink.

"Yes, not stealing anything or shooting up." I pause for a heartbeat and continue. "My friend's dad translated. 'Fuyi' means lucky in art or something like that."

Mom's mouth straightens. "Yes, well, the orphanage just made that one up. They needed to call you something while you lived there. And put something on the papers."

"Really?"

"Of course. If your parents had left a name, they might as well have come forward and formally put you up for adoption, instead of . . ." She flounders for a moment.

"Abandoning me by a lamppost at the back door of the nursery?" I finish for her. It's a punch in the gut. Even this name that doesn't suit me doesn't come from my real parents. It feels as if I have nothing of my own.

"Oh, honey. It's just the best they could do under impossible circumstances. They knew you'd be found there. If they had come forward, they would have been fined."

"So they'd get some kind of ticket for putting me up for adoption?"

"For having you in the first place!" my mother says. "A fine would have broken a poor family. We can't imagine it. We're never even hungry, never mind starving."

She's right. I can't imagine it. How is it possible for people on one side of the world to be so poor that they throw their children away? I can't let myself feel sad or I will be swallowed. Instead, I tuck myself behind a shell. I straighten my shoulders, hold my mouth in a neutral line and breathe deeply.

"Paige, Paige, don't hate her." Mom rushes to hug me again. "I only wish I could contact your mother to thank her for what she's done for us. Because of her sacrifice, we have you." Mom's crying.

From behind my shell, it's hard to reach around her and hug back. Finally, I speak again. "Why did you call me Paige?" A silly question, the answer can't solve anything.

"We just thought the name sounded pretty."

"You didn't hope I'd be a writer?" I ask her.

"Heavens, no." She smiles. "If anything, I knew bringing you home was turning a wonderful page in our life." She hugs me so tightly that I can smell the salt of her tears. "But it's the wrong spelling, in any case."

"What's in a name?" I repeat Juliet's and Max's dad's words and shrug, relieved I haven't disappointed her in how I turned out.

"We should go to China together. You need to be astounded and amazed, and then you won't hate your birth country and family so much."

I shake my head. "I just can't." I want to feel something besides this rockiness in my chest. With only five days left, there isn't enough time to visit my homeland, even if I can stomach it. No time, unless I somehow shift occurrences enough . . . but won't Kim and her elders have to reel me back to that beach in the sky if I change things that drastically? Have I changed anything based on knowledge gained from my previous week? How can I not have caused different things to happen? I'm behaving differently, and yet I'm still here. There has to be hope.

Thursday's Field Trip

∞

Next morning, we're off to the science center for our field trip. Fifty-four kids fit on a bus, which means both our grade nine classes squeeze together in that enclosed area. Windows are shut and frosted over, so we can't even see outside. The smell of wet coats and cherry bubble gum overwhelms me, and because there doesn't seem to be anywhere else to look, my eyes drift to the new official couple.

They come out in a big way: beautiful and in a world of their own, like actors in a perfume commercial. Jazz leans her head full of shiny black hair on Cameron's shoulder. He strokes it, strokes her face and kisses her. Their love doesn't seem like a game he's playing to make Vanessa jealous. Something temporary. It looks gentle and sweet, a real feeling that's growing bigger.

Doesn't everyone want to experience love like that?

Certainly I do. Instead, I sit next to Max, the round-faced boy with the square bangs. That feels easy and comfortable, like sitting on a blanket on the beach. Not that beach where Kim is waiting for me, though.

In the seat ahead of us, Vanessa sits alone with her forehead pressed against the frozen window. She hasn't even rubbed a looking hole out of the white. I can smell her burnt-tire anger, like a car accident when the driver desperately brakes.

Max chatters at me about the things he found out about the exhibit, when he searched for it on the Internet last night. Apparently Gunther von Hagens is the one who devised the plastination method to preserve the entire body from the inside out. "The idea came to him at the butcher. He decided to try the same meat slicer on a human liver. Which made it way easier to cut it all up and saturate it with polymer."

Vanessa turns around. "You're making me sick; why don't you just shut up?"

My mouth drops open—I can't help but gape. She looks pale and she isn't wearing any makeup. What's up with her? Does she think she can entice Cameron back with her white eyelashes and faded eyes?

She snaps around in her seat again to sulk at the pane full of frost.

Max stops talking and wags his eyebrows at me to make fun of Vanessa. Still, he clams up as she commanded, and really, what could she do to make him? Somehow he knows enough not to cross her. I wish he had the courage to stand up to her. Then I would know I can count on him. Besides, I really want to know more about von Hagens's procedure.

It takes about forty-five minutes to get to the science center. When the bus rolls to a stop by the student entrance, we file out. Seat by seat. Vanessa, Abbi, Kierstead and a couple of other volleyball girls hang together.

We stay clear of them as we stroll through the grand hall to the Body Worlds exhibit. Max continues his explanation about how von Hagens devised ways to suck out all the fat and water from a body. And how he experimented with combinations of rubber, epoxy and polyester, injecting them in to preserve not just one organ but entire corpses. "After he fills them with the plastic, he just positions the body however he wants it and lets it harden. The whole process takes about fifteen hundred hours."

We arrive at the entrance to the exhibition, where there's a large sign warning that photography is strictly forbidden. Around the corner sits a man, head leaning against his hand, as though he's thinking. Only he has no skin or hair. His eyeballs look weird, bulging, and his irises are blue, contrasting sharply with the red of his plastinated flesh. According to the write-up on the wall next to him, the eyeballs are the only artificial things about any of the displays. Herr von Hagens can't find a way to preserve them.

Vanessa hangs back, but Mr. Brewster catches her. "Do I have to go in? I'm not feeling good," she tells him.

You can see he's torn. He has to think for a moment.

"I can stay with her," Kierstead offers, twirling a strand of hair around her finger.

"Me, too," Abbi says.

Too many girls surround him; he backs away. "No, you can't all miss this exhibit. This is a once-in-a-lifetime opportunity." He takes Vanessa by the elbow. "Come inside the room at least. You don't have to look at the bodies, but I need to know what you're doing."

I shake my head at Max as we brush past them. Ahead of us the royal couple stands admiring the first display, a body riding a stallion. The skinned horse rears up on its hind legs, and its front legs claw at the air with a lot of attitude. For a dead horse, that is.

Jasmine points to the stallion's flank, where a missing slice of flesh reveals the stomach and intestines. Cameron gestures to the riding crop clenched in the bony fingers of the rider. He's split into two halves for us all to view his insides. Jazz and Cameron look happy and cozy holding hands as they gaze in wonder at the cadavers.

Both as one, they murmur, "Cool, eh?" to Max and me as we scoot ahead of them.

We check out the athlete cadavers on display. Lots of muscles and sinews. Some exposed organs. "Look at how intricate the veins are," I say. I like the look of determination on their faces.

We also see an ape. Apart from the head, which looks distinctively monkey-shaped, and the thighs, so much heavier with muscle than those of the human athletes, the rest of the body seems very Homo sapiens. A really good exhibit to argue for evolution. Max takes out his cell phone and snaps a photo of the skinned ape.

"You know you're not allowed to take pictures," I tell him.

"As long as I don't sell them, nobody's going to say anything," he answers.

I look around. No white coats come rushing for us. "Gee, I wouldn't mind having some photos of all this. It's great."

"I'll send you some."

Next up is a woman sitting, looking very relaxed for a corpse with her belly cut open. The opening in her body allows us to see her fetus. I don't feel sad about the possibilities that ended for this person or her child. Even the first time through this exhibit, without Max, I felt detached. Which would have been a good thing if I could have carried out my plans for life. I wanted to go into research eventually.

Now, knowing that the real essence of me can interact with Kimberly on a beach, while my body sleeps on a hospital bed, makes me even more detached.

Still, I do feel a tiny prickle of sadness at the thought that I will never carry a baby the way this woman did. For that matter, I will never carry one in my arms, either. I didn't even know I wanted to have kids till I looked at the thirty-three-week-old fetus. Perfect little toes, perfect fingers— only something obviously went wrong in its life. It was cheated of even more possibilities than I have been. I hear some squeals and turn around.

In the center of the room is an exhibit that attracts a crowd of our classmates. "Come on. Let's check it out," Max says.

We can't make out what the draw is till we push closer. Morgan giggles nervously as I squeeze in beside her. There, crouching in front of us, a man and a woman seem oddly joined together.

"They're having sex," Gwyn says as though she's disgusted.

"It's not like it was their choice," Emma answers her. "Somebody just posed them like that."

"Why would anyone let someone do that to them?" Morgan asks.

"For science," I answer.

"They donate their bodies. Look on that wall; the donor form is there," Max tells her.

I frown. I would have donated my body to science if someone had asked me. Only I would have liked control of how I was displayed. For sure not like this couple in front of us.

Vanessa still drifts around, almost ghostlike. As we move away from the couple, she moves in.

Mr. Brewster directs us to a cart covered with a white cloth. It looks like some serving cart for a fancy dinner, only sitting on this tablecloth are organs.

"Go ahead. Pick one up," the girl in the lab coat says. "Sarah," her name-tag reads.

Max grins as he picks up a dark brown half-moon. "It

feels like Plasticine when you've left it out too long." He passes it to me.

"That's a liver," Sarah tells us. "What do you think this is?" She hands me an off-white slab of meat with a tube coming from its side.

I squeeze. It feels spongy, like a Nerf organ.

She gives Max one that looks gray and black. "Here's a big hint. That one belongs to a smoker," she tells him.

"Lungs," I answer.

"Imagine breathing through it. Like inhaling through charcoal." Max's eyes bug.

Sarah raises her eyebrows. "Can't feel great."

Someone shoves into me. "This is just a stupid display," Vanessa snaps. "My grandmother and grandfather smoke. They're like a hundred years old."

"Maybe the smoking only makes them look a hundred years old," Max suggests.

I grin. "Yeah, smoking does cause wrinkles."

Vanessa's eyes narrow as she gives me her killer look.

Okay, bad move teasing her. She has no sense of humor. Still, how can anyone think that purposely inhaling burning anything wouldn't be harmful?

Max and I drift away, looking at more bodies and organs and even the veins in a brain. Fascinating stuff.

Before we leave the exhibit, I head for the washroom, happy to have cruised through Body Worlds twice in one week (if you count my last lifetime). Safe and sitting anonymously inside a stall, I hear Vanessa come in crying.

"Not everyone gets lung cancer," I hear Kierstead tell her.

"My mother smokes," Vanessa sobs. "She's done it since she was twelve. So she's got those black lungs."

I hear Vanessa blow her nose, and I flush and step out of my stall. Last time through this week, I might have stayed hidden in there till they left.

"Lung cancer isn't the only problem smoking causes," I tell her as I wash my hands.

"Shut up," Kierstead snaps at me. "Can't you see she's upset?"

But as I pull the paper towel from the dispenser, I continue nonchalantly, "There's emphysema and cardiovascular disease." I saw them all hanging out at the far edge of the football field, Vanessa and her team members, puffing their lungs out. I know Vanessa isn't only worried about her mom or her grandparents. "Really, Vanessa, you should quit smoking."

"Easy for you to say; you're a toothpick."

"Take up jogging. Better for volleyball than smoking." *Too cocky?* I turn to head out the door.

Kierstead steps in front of me. "You're such a snot, you know that?" Bared teeth and wrinkled nose, her face looms ugly in front of mine, all her faked sweet silliness gone.

I speak into that anger. "Within twenty minutes of your last cigarette, your body starts to heal itself. Your skin will improve. Your breath will, too."

"Think you're so smart!" Kierstead shoves me hard against the wall.

I feel my ribs crunch. Amazing how much it hurts, considering I never felt the train throw me. I slide down. It isn't the pain, it's the fear of what will come that is the worst.

By the time my butt touches the floor, I think, no matter what, I'm not going to live this week cowering. So I take a breath and speak at Vanessa. "If your mom quits, her risk of heart attack will drop within twenty-four hours." I peel myself away from the wall and off the floor, staggering to my feet. "After forty-eight hours, her nerve endings will repair themselves."

Vanessa raises a fist and I duck around her, grabbing hold of the door handle.

"All I'm saying is that it's not too late for any of you." I quickly pull at it and slip out.

"Over here," Max calls. "What's wrong with you? You look funny."

I hold my ribs. "Nothing. Just told Vanessa she should quit smoking."

"Oh man, do you have a death wish or something?" He grabs my arm and drags me away quickly.

"No, definitely not. Dying is something I really don't want to do right now."

RETAKE:

Thursday after School

∞

By the time we walk home that afternoon, the snow has turned crunchy again. The cold air stings our faces like a slap—even Jazz's cheeks turn pink—and I find myself looking over my shoulder.

I'm supposed to help my best friend against those hard-eyed jocks. But not only did she flaunt her happiness in Vanessa's face, I also gave out health lectures in the washroom. Surely, between the two of us, we bumped up our date with the volleyball team. Will they catch up with us at the overpass today instead of Monday?

Jazz doesn't notice me speeding up our walk. She just prattles away in faster white-puff breaths about the exhibit. "Did you see they had the donor form on the wall display? Can you imagine wanting to donate your body after seeing the exhibit?"

"Yeah." To study biology, I would have had to look at some donor's cadaver one day. I frown as I think about all the diseases I won't be able to find the cure for, the discoveries I'll never make. Before that day on the train track, I hadn't even thought about dying, let alone donating any part of my body.

"It's so dehumanizing. A real person becomes a posable statue," Jazz continues.

"It helps educate the public. Wouldn't you donate your body for science?" I ask.

"And have some medical students laugh at my lack of boobs? No way."

"Think of it differently. Because of your body, some doctor will learn how to save someone else."

"Since when did you become so noble? They're going to cut the body up."

"Worms are going to eat you, anyway. Or maybe someone will cremate you; there's not enough room on the planet to bury everyone under a nice tombstone." It's time for Jazz to turn off the route toward her house.

"True." Jazz stops for a moment, then touches my shoulder with her mittened hand. "Thanks, Paige."

"For what?" I'm anxious to get out of the volleyball team's range of revenge. "I didn't do anything."

"Yeah. Because of you I can at least pretend my life is normal."

It's one of those mushy moments that I used to hate because I didn't understand them before my train accident. Today, I really want to try. But I glance over my shoulder and see people in the distance. "You're my only friend, too," I tell her back. "Now can we just hurry home where it's warm? We can chat later on Facebook."

She grins and nods, and we go our separate ways.

I run the rest of the way home, hoping she does the same. Who knows when Vanessa might jump out at either of us. Phew! When I step into the warmth of our house, I hang up my coat, kick off my boots and head straight for the computer in the den to do homework.

Of course, I check Facebook first and see that Max has posted photos of Body Worlds. Too cool. I grin as I click on each picture and see, one by one, Max's favorites. I download a copy of each to my hard drive. He's even taken one of that intertwined couple. I click "Like." In a few moments, another comment appears.

Jasmine Aggarwal: How did you take these? I thought no photos were allowed.

As big a nerd as I am, she's on her computer the second she gets in the door, too.

I answer with two words—Cell phone—and then don't think anything more about it as I finish my homework.

When Dad comes home, I help him make chili, crumbling up the little package of ground soy into the frying pan. "How was your science trip?" he asks.

"It was really great. Dead people sculptures. Would you

donate your body to science?" I ask as I stir in the beans.

"No," he says flatly as he dumps in a can of chopped tomatoes.

"What about organs?" I sample the chili and hold out the spoon for him to taste. "Wouldn't you donate your heart for Mom?"

His lips curl upward only slightly. "I already have." He brings the spoon to his mouth and tastes the chili. "It's missing something. Pass me the cumin." He shakes some in. "Chili powder." He holds out his hand like a surgeon waiting for a tool. I pass him the chili powder and he sprinkles it in.

"So you would donate your heart? What about your lungs, your pancreas, your eyes, your liver and your kidneys?"

"Donating an organ for your mother is different. For you, too. Heck, I'd give you a kidney while I'm still alive." He tosses a dash of hot sauce into the chili. "But for someone I don't know . . ." He shakes his head and tastes the chili again, making a face. "A dash of cinnamon, maybe."

I reach into the cupboard and hand him some. "But you know that I want to study biology, and I need bodies for that."

"Look, can we not talk about this anymore?"

But we talk about everything, I want to argue. That's what Mom always says. Only Dad rarely raises an eyebrow, never mind his voice. Today I hear an edge, maybe even a splintering in his words. If I ask anything more about organs, I think he might crack open. *A touchy subject?*

Too bad, because I remember about Kim's parents asking for donations to the Kidney Foundation at the end of her obituary.

When Mom gets home, I follow her up to their bedroom and ask her as soon as we're alone, "Mom, you know I saw Kim Ellis's obituary on the Net. Why did her parents ask for donations to the Kidney Foundation?"

Mom looks as though she's trying to swallow her mouth. *Painful memories?* I wonder. Finally, she speaks. "Well, you know when you have a bacterial infection, the kidney is the worst place for it to hit really badly. Kim ate that bad hamburger and the *E. coli* attacked her kidney."

"Makes sense. They couldn't really ask for donations to the better hamburger fund, I guess."

"No, but they could have asked for them for Sick Kids Hospital." Mom seems almost angry for a moment. I want to ask her more questions but don't even know exactly what answers I'm looking for.

"Look, Kim's death was a real shock to us." Mom pulls off her Foods R Good shirt. "We never really got over it."

"No kidding. Dad doesn't even want to talk about organ donation."

"Well, then, just leave it alone, Paige." She pulls on a lime green T-shirt with white handprints all over it. My handprints. I'd decorated it about three years ago for Mother's Day and she still wears it. "Try to be sensitive to other people's feelings."

It feels a lot like that sting of cold air across my face on my way home this afternoon. I look at her sideways. "Mom, can I say one thing before we drop it?"

She looks me in the eye. "Go ahead."

"If something should happen to me . . ." I stare back into those blue eyes that are so electrically charged and sensitive to my moods. I want to tell her *Please, please pull the plug, because if I can't live my life, I should at least be able to live out my afterlife.* Kim and I should be able to move on.

Or we'll be stuck on a beach forever.

But I would only be asking because I know that if fate plays out exactly the same way, I will be rigged to some kind of ventilator by Monday night.

Surely that's against the rules—to ask to be released because of my prior knowledge. So I start again, on something I've always wanted but just never mentioned. "If something should happen to me, I want you to donate all my organs. My eyes, my lungs, my liver, my kidneys . . ."

She chokes back a sob then and looks away from me. That one word "kidneys" has upset her. Probably something to do with Kim.

"Aw, Mom. We're talking recycling here." I try to kid her out of her tears. "Just don't let anything go to waste. That's all I'm asking."

Mom bows her head and holds the bridge between her brows with two fingers. Her shoulders shake.

RETAKE:

Friday Morning

∞

Next day, the same snow flurries that occurred last Friday keep Dad back from the food terminal again. Mom and Dad decide to take the van in together and, if business is quiet, they will shut the store early.

Before they leave, I make sure to give them each a big hug.

"Mmm, this is nice," Mom says. "To what do we owe this?"

"Growing up?" I suggest.

"Sometimes it has its advantages," Dad says as he kisses my forehead.

If my previous destiny cannot be altered, there isn't too much time left. I watch as Mom's van backs out of the driveway and I wave. Then I swallow hard and head off, too.

Feathers of white swirl around me as I wait at the corner for Jazz. She must be running late. I turn to her house so we won't miss one of our last walks to school together.

"Sorry, I slept in. Just be a sec." She opens the door wider, and I step into the entrance of a whole different world, one that manages to surprise me all over again each time I visit Jazz.

The furniture looks large and overstuffed, bright green and red, with a huge leather footstool and a dark wooden elephant coffee table. This morning, the air smells like an exotic dinner. Hints of garlic and cumin make my mouth water. A different exotic world.

Jazz dashes from her room with her backpack. "See you later, Mom," she calls as she slips into her coat.

Her mother comes quickly to the door, smiling. With the same green eyes as Jasmine, she has the same warm brown skin, too, only on her it looks so much more foreign. Like all of Jasmine's family.

"Don't forget, I'll be home late. Paige and I are helping Mrs. Falkner in the library today."

"It is very nice of you girls to help your teacher so much." She tips her head and Jazz brushes her lips across her cheeks. "And, Paige, you will be coming to Beena's party on Saturday, yes?"

Last time her mother invited me, I made the excuse that I needed to help my parents in the store. Seeing all that extended family partying could be depressing. This time, I smile. "Thank you, yes. I wouldn't miss it."

"Very well. We will be seeing you." Her mother continues to watch us as we step to the end of the walkway, then waves from the window.

Because of the snow, the cold has cracked open to a softer warmer temperature. I look up at the sky. White everywhere. Beneath our boots, the snow feels wet and clumpy, perfect for snowballs or short-lived snowmen.

At the end of the block, I look back, and Mrs. Aggarwal is still there. I can just make out her bright red sari.

"They don't give me a minute of freedom," Jazz complains through gritted teeth, picking up some snow and forming it into a ball.

"She's so proud of you," I say. But I know firsthand what that kind of adoration does to you. It weighs you down with expectations, makes it hard to breathe. Makes it hard for them to pull the plug and let you give up your breath. I try not to think about how this all will end on Monday. The closer it draws, the more difficult that becomes.

"As long as I do everything her way, she'll stay proud." Jazz throws the snowball hard onto a stop sign so that the *O* is filled in with white. She pauses to admire it, then turns to me. "Thanks for backing me up."

"No problem." We slop through the soft snow to the school, then climb the stairs to the front door. I push it open, and we both stomp our boots on the mat in the foyer. Just ahead, people gather around the trophy case next to the office, but we continue straight ahead for our lockers. Something white flashes at us from Jazz's door.

When we draw closer, we can see it's an enlarged photo of the intertwined couple from Body Worlds. Only the heads don't belong to any red-veined cadavers; they are Jazz's and Cameron's, cut and pasted onto the bodies.

Jazz gasps. We both freeze for a moment, then she rips the picture from her locker.

But I get a sinking feeling. The crowd at the trophy case. "Let's go back to the office."

Sure enough, stuck to the glass pane is another poster. I tear this down for Jazz. She looks like she's hyperventilating.

"It's just a stupid picture. Don't let it get to you," I tell her.

"If my mother sees one of these," she gasps, "I'm dead."

"Relax. We took them all down." When we step into the washroom to give Jazz a chance to calm down, we see that all the mirrors have the posters on them, too. Jazz tears them off frantically. I try to help but she's faster.

"It's not your fault someone fooled around with Photoshop. Your mother can't blame you," I tell her when she starts to cry.

"She'll figure out that something's going on between me and Cameron. She'll tell my father."

I help her shred the photos into the trash. "Don't worry, they'll never see these."

I stay with her as she washes her face with cold water, hopeful that Vanessa has done her worst. Then we head to homeroom a few minutes late. For me, it's English with Mrs. Corbin. No one gives me any grief about slipping in after the bell. Emma doesn't shove any notes in my hand, and Zoe and Gwyn seem to be paying attention to Shakespeare.

No gym today, so the morning goes smoothly. Jazz spends lunch hour with Cameron as usual, and I hang out with Max, who buys me a chicken wiener in the cafeteria. When we finish eating, I go with him to Mr. Brewster's lab to help him set up for an experiment. I like that. It isn't Disney World—or even Canada's Wonderland-exciting for my second-last day at school—but it's nice. I don't even see Vanessa or any of her followers.

Then, a few minutes before dismissal, the intercom snaps on. "Your attention, please. Would Paige Barta and Max Liu report to the front office?"

Sitting next to me, Jazz turns my way and raises her eyebrows.

I shrug. This is a new one on me, too. So much changes just because I ate that hamburger with Max on Monday. "Probably a slipup on attendance," I explain as I stand up. The teacher watches as I head off. I'm curious but not really worried.

Till I sit with Max across from Mrs. Norr and she slaps down the Photoshopped picture of the intertwined cadavers. She pushes it toward us over the expanse of desk and papers.

"Who do you think is responsible for this?" Mrs. Norr asks.

"Not us," Max sputters.

"You were spotted taking photos in Body Worlds. Did you know that pictures were not permitted?"

Not saying a word, Max lowers his head and nods.

"Paige, did you know Max was taking photos?"

"Yes." I don't add anything like "I told him not to." I don't want to get him into even more trouble.

"Did he post this photo on Facebook?"

"No, of course not."

"Did he post any of the Body Worlds photos on Facebook?"

I glance at Max and feel my skin get hot. He isn't the one who put Cameron's and Jazz's heads on the passionate dead couple. He doesn't have any reason to make fun of them. But who are his other Facebook friends?

"Let me ask you again, who do you think is responsible for this piece of work?"

Honestly, does Mrs. Norr really not know what is going on? "Vanessa McDonald," I finally tell her.

Max's eyes widen and his eyebrows make a leap for his bangs. He looks shocked that I would give up her name.

"And what evidence do you have?" Mrs. Norr asks.

"Nothing. Except she's really mad about Jasmine going out with her former boyfriend."

"Well, that's extremely interesting, Paige. Because Vanessa is the one who brought this . . . ," she lifts up the Photoshopped masterpiece, "to my attention. She told me about Max's photos on Facebook."

"Of course she did," I grumble. You have to hand it to Vanessa, she really knows how to stir up the toilet bowl.

"I will have Mrs. Spence draw up a letter for you to deliver to your parents. As of right now, you are both suspended."

"What? But, Mrs. Norr, Paige didn't have anything to do with this. I was the one who took the pictures."

"I'm going to call all the parents involved." She picks up her phone.

Max's head pitches forward and he closes his eyes.

I fold my arms across my chest. *Kicked out of school!* How will this all work out fate-wise? On Monday I won't even be walking home, never mind detouring by the train track. And then I begin to breathe faster—who is Mrs. Norr calling?

"You may wait outside." She gestures with her fingers for us to leave.

Max scrapes back his chair as he stands. I follow more slowly, still in shock. As I step out of her office, I hear Mrs. Norr speaking into the phone. "Yes, Mrs. Aggarwal. I'm sorry to disturb you, but there's been a bit of an incident at school, and we would like to discuss it with you and your husband in person."

Friday Afternoon

∞

O f course she would call Jazz's parents first! The bell rings and I turn to Max. "I'm not hanging around for the letter. I have to warn Jazz her parents are coming." I don't wait for Max's answer, just dash out of the office to catch Jazz before she leaves on her date. Kids empty into the hall, swarming the lockers. I weave and dodge as quickly as possible to my own. *Don't be gone yet, don't be gone yet.*

The love couple walks toward the door.

"Jazz, wait!" I wave and catch up to her. "Something's happened. I've been suspended."

"What?"

"Let's keep walking as we talk. Mrs. Norr knows about those photos. She thinks Max and I made them."

"That's ridiculous," Cameron says. "This is so Vanessa."

"Yeah, well, it gets worse."

"How?" Jazz looks scared. She has to have guessed already.

"She's calling in everyone's parents." I bite my lip. "Everyone's. Victims', too."

"But she can't. Let's go back and talk to her. Between us, we can convince her. If she talks to Mom and Dad, I'll be on a plane to India next week."

"Jazz, please." I try to talk softly, to soothe her. "Don't go all nutso over this. I couldn't head Mrs. Norr off in time. She already reached your mother."

"What?" Jasmine's jaw drops. Her eyes scream.

"Yeah, that's why I wanted to grab you before you went to the mall. She might be on her way to the school right this minute."

"Oh my gawd. Cameron, you have to leave!" She begins pushing at him.

"Come on, Jazz." He catches her hands. "Why don't we just face her together?"

"No, no." She begins hammering at his chest. "I can't."

"Sooner or later, you knew your parents had to find out about me," he reasons.

"Go, go, go!" she sobs hysterically.

I put my hands on her shoulders and pull her away from Cameron, wincing at him. "She needs to tell her mom on her own."

Cameron throws up his hands helplessly. He reaches for Jazz but she pulls away. "Jazz, let me talk to your parents. You'll see. We can make this all right."

Who knew that Cameron could be such a stand-up kind of guy? Hanging around Vanessa had hidden all his better qualities.

"I'll call you. Okay?" His eyes plead with her.

She shakes her head, all the while holding it in both hands. "You have to go now!" she tells him in a panicked voice.

He looks worse than when Vanessa slapped him. His brow furrows, his mouth crumples. Then he just walks away, out the door.

"No, no, no!" Jasmine wails.

"Calm down, Jazz. It's going to be all right." I talk softly, evenly.

"My mother's going to come here with Dad and head straight for the library to find me!"

"Well, let's just go there ourselves. You can help me shut the computers down." I tug Jazz toward the resource room. She's a mess. How will I explain her state to Mrs. Falkner?

Inside the library, I call out hello to the librarian, who's working at her desk in her office. "Is it still snowing? I thought we would let out early."

Mrs. Falkner stands up and peers out the window. "Looks like it let up."

"I brought Jasmine to help. We'll get the computers, okay?" I push Jazz to the bank of PCs closest to the wall just in case one of the volleyball team posted some nasty notes early. If Jazz sees an ambush plan, maybe she will want to wait for her mom and dad to drive us home. There may be worse things than a quick visit to India; facing the volleyball team could be one of them. "Breathe, Jasmine!"

She looks at me, her face so drained, her hair ragged from pulling at it.

"Or Mrs. Falkner will want to know what's up."

Jazz nods.

"Make sure to check the screens and save the students' work." Coming from me, she should find that command odd.

But I have to give her credit. Despite everything, she goes to work. One computer, two, the next one would have been the one. She doesn't seem any more upset as she checks out the screen.

I dash over just to make sure. No Facebook showing on it. Has Vanessa satisfied her lust for revenge with those posters? Or will they just gang up on us on Monday as they'd planned before?

Jazz's eyes keep checking the door, maybe for her parents. Finally, the last computer powers down.

"Do you mind shelving these before you go?" Mrs. Falkner asks.

I steal a quick look at the clock. We've been here twenty minutes already. "But it's the weekend!" I say.

"That's why I want the library tidy. There are only ten books, but I'll do it if you want to leave," Mrs. Falkner says.

"No, we'll help!" Jazz insists. "That way we can all get going." Her eyes signal me to hurry. She wants Mrs. Falkner gone in case her parents check with her on the supposed volunteer work. So we both get busy. By the time the books are away, the snow starts again. "Look, Mrs. F, that storm's coming after all!"

"You're right. I'm leaving, too." She grabs her coat.

I can hear Jazz sigh with relief. One of her lies will not be immediately uncovered.

As fast as I can, I grab my coat and books from the locker. Jazz already has hers. "You can come to my house," I say to her as we move. "Everything's going to be fine. You'll see."

I don't know what else to say. I've never seen Jasmine so wild-eyed and frantic.

"Maybe we should walk along the tracks," Jasmine says as we step out the door. "I don't want to see my parents. I can't think of what I'm going to say to them."

"I . . . I don't know." Snow drifts down a little quicker now. What if all the scheduled weather and events are pushed just slightly off-kilter? Still, even if a train comes, we should be fine. With no earbuds in or music pounding, I will hear it. Maybe the two of us together will be safe from the bullies and the train. But in my head I hear the short note of the train's cry, then the long desperate one, and freeze. "I can't," I finally say, squeezing my eyes shut.

"Can you at least hurry!" Jazz rips at my arm and marches me along.

We head for the overpass. Above the tracks, I have to be safe; no need for my knees to wobble. The wind begins to whirl the snow around us.

Heads down, we trudge up the incline. "We'll have a sleepover tonight. Your mom will say yes to that, right? You can talk to my parents." I babble on at Jasmine. She doesn't respond. I don't know what is going through her head.

"Hey! Browner girls!" a voice calls from behind us. *Kierstead?*

Ice shoots up my spine. "Faster," I tell Jasmine. We break into a run.

Something hits the back of my head hard. Ow! A snowball? I touch the sore spot where it landed, pull my hand away and see blood. A rock must have been rolled into that snow.

"Banana's not brown. She's yellow." Vanessa's rasp.

Jazz slips then. I crouch to help her even as I see the bunch of them run up the overpass toward us.

I get Jasmine up.

"You're going to pay for stealing my boyfriend," Vanessa hisses.

"Don't listen, just keep going," I tell Jazz.

She shakes her head and stops.

I hear the train clanging its warning bell as it heads toward the overpass.

Jazz scrambles up the hand railing. We're up about three stories. Even if she lands in the snow, there's a chance she might not make it.

"Don't, Jazz. You'll hurt yourself!" I cry. But in her green eyes I see a final calmness. She doesn't care, I realize. I hesitate for a moment. *This can't happen,* I decide. *This is not what I came back for.* So as she lifts off, I dive forward to grab her back.

A second too late.

My fingers catch the tail of her coat. I feel my nails bend as I struggle to hold on. But the coat yanks away. This is all happening differently. Three days earlier than last time. I have another split second to decide what to do.

If I stay behind, maybe I will alter destiny enough and stay alive.

I stare at the angry girls heading my way. I returned to Earth to stand up for Jasmine. Now it looks like I need to save her from herself instead.

Kim didn't abandon me all those years ago; it's more like our family abandoned her. This time there is no excuse. I climb the railing and aim for a snowdrift, then jump. I land on my feet in the deep soft snow. Jasmine lies in front of me across the metal rails. I can hear the frantic short horn note and then the long one. I pull myself out of the bank and dash to grab Jazz. I grab at her arm, throwing myself backward, getting us both out of the way in time. At least I hope.

But, instead, everything goes black.

Back at the Beach

∞

The sun feels hotter on my shoulders this time; the wind's breath blows harder. The waves pound the shore with a *rush, rush* sound. The palm trees swing their necks in the wind like they're shaking their heads, *No. No. Wrong!*

A tall girl stands staring out at the horizon. Her long black hair hangs smooth and straight like a silk scarf. She wears a white one-piece swimsuit that is cut to make her legs and arms look even longer and thinner. The white glows against her skin, which is a light brown, on the golden side. She turns to face me. "You're here early this time." She sounds happy, as though she was waiting for me to get there.

It makes me want to hug and protect her against the loneliness. "Where's Kim?" I ask.

This girl has hardly any brows, but her brown eyes hold a depth, her smile carries a sad warmth.

Something about her seems familiar. I feel a pull inside me.

"Don't you like me this way?" her voice asks me in teenager whine.

She looks like someone I know but not Kim. I squint at her.

She grabs my glasses from me. "I don't know why you wear these. You could have asked your mom for contact lenses." She puts them on herself.

And I gasp.

It's like looking in the mirror.

"Still don't recognize your best friend?"

"Kim?" *What about Jasmine? How has she made out?* I wonder. *Did I push her far enough out of the way?* "You can't be Kim. She's only seven years old."

"Now I'm fourteen." She grins.

"In five days, you aged seven years?"

"I asked to. I wanted to stay your best friend. No fourteen-year-old wants to hang around with a little kid."

"Did you have them make you look exactly like me?" Me and yet somehow prettier. Or could I actually be that good-looking, too?

"You know what they say. All Asians look alike."

"No, Kim. They don't."

"We always looked the same."

I reach back in my mind for a visual memory. Seven years is such a long time ago. "Our moms used to dress us the same. People got us mixed up."

"That's right. You remember!"

There is something odd about that, but I can't put my finger on it. Maybe it's this whole experience, like a vivid nightmare. "What happened to Jasmine? Did I save her?"

"You didn't even ask about her last time," Kim scolds. "It was all about you."

I think about that for a moment. "But she wasn't with me on the train track!"

"Yes, but those girls were going to ambush her on the overpass and you weren't there to help her."

"Okay, you're right. It was all about me last time. But I want to know about her today: Was she hurt?"

"Not last time. But today she's dead." She says it so matter-of-factly, I can't believe it for a moment.

"No!" I tell her as though scolding a bad dog. "Why isn't she here with us, then?"

"You're not in the same category. You're only mostly dead. Your mother still has to pull the plug." She stares at me, her head tilted. I see that she can't understand my disbelief. To her, being dead is everyday life.

I also see that she's telling me the straight-up truth. "Kimmee!" I sink to my knees, the hot sand scorching them. "I can't have killed her by going back!"

"No, you didn't." She smiles at me. "She made the choice to jump."

"But it was all because of those stupid pictures." I stare at the sun-bright diamonds of sand for a moment, then stagger back up to my feet. "It didn't happen when I walked around Body Worlds all by myself."

"True." Kim just looks at me, owl-like through my glasses.

I pull them off her and put them back on. "So I try to be a better person, and I end up making things worse?"

She shrugs. "These things never work out all that well."

"Can I go back? I didn't get a full week."

"But you don't know what the outcome will be this time, either."

"She can't die because of some stupid Facebook photos." I grab Kim's arms. "Get me back to Body Worlds. Only one extra day."

Kim rolls her eyes, and it's so eerie. I saw that exact facial expression in my mother's dresser mirror when I rolled my own eyes at something she said. I can't process how bizarre having a doppelgänger is just at that moment. I have to concentrate on saving Jazz. "Kim, please?"

"I'll check." She jogs into the water, deeper and deeper. When the waves reach her armpits, she throws her arms open into a breaststroke and disappears.

I stare after her for a moment, then down at my feet. This time there is no castle to build, no hole to dig or parents to search for at the other end of the hole. I lift my eyes again toward those waving palm trees. I breathe in the slightly off smell of the seaweed at the edge of the beach and watch two seagulls dip and dive into the ocean. They call to each other in a high worried pitch.

I look down to the point on the ocean where Kim disappeared.

Still no Kim.

It's taking so much longer this time. All I really need to do is snatch Max's phone from him at Body Worlds so he can't take photos. It won't even take the whole day. They can suck me right from the face of the planet after that moment. I wish I could tell them this myself.

What is taking Kim so long? She isn't a great person to argue my case. She's always been kind of an all-logic, no-emotion kid. Just like me.

Maybe that's the way all babies left under lampposts grow up to be. But why does she look so much like me? Does your personality shape the way your cheeks and nose form? Or is that our Chinese heritage?

At last, I see the air sparkle as though diamonds of sand have been tossed into it. The sparkle turns into gold and finally Kim forms. She walks toward me.

"Okay," she says tiredly. "You get to go back again." She beckons with her hand, and I wade into the ocean to meet her. Then she grabs me and shoves my head under the water.

Third Time a Charm

∞

When I surface, I'm strolling through Body Worlds with Max. We're heading to the ape cadaver, and he reaches into his pocket.

"Don't take a picture," I say.

"How did you know what I was going to do?" Max asks.

"Well, I didn't think you needed to make a phone call." I put my hand on his wrist.

His skin flushes. He smiles at me. "Fine, I won't take a photo. I would have sent you a copy."

"My mother gave me some extra money. Why don't we just go to the souvenir shop? Maybe we can buy a plastic kidney or something instead."

"Sure." He slips his wrist from under my hand and grabs mine. Something really strange happens then. He leans over and kisses me. Not on the cheek, either. It isn't a long, passionate, tonsil-hockey kind of smooch. His lips touch mine so quickly that I can almost swear it never happened.

My second kiss from a boy, both from him. He's just a friend, a fairly dorky-looking one at that. But he makes me want to live longer so that I can experience the real thing someday.

He doesn't say anything, just tugs me along to the next exhibit. Everything else pretty much happens the same way, except that, after the washroom break, we head for the gift shop and I buy a couple of postcards for us. I keep the one of the horseback rider. The other, a shot of the ape cadaver, I give to him. Nobody would bother to Photoshop Jazz's or Cameron's head onto either one.

That afternoon, on the walk home from school, I feel just as tense as if I had read a Facebook plan to beat us up at the overpass. Events keep shifting. The last time, the volleyball team ambushed us three days early; maybe it would be four this time.

Jazz and I have the conversation about organ donation with me checking over my shoulder. I walk more slowly despite the cold.

"Jazz, have you ever talked to your mother about guys?"

"Gawd no. As it is, my grandfather will be sending photos of suitable boys."

"Don't you wonder if your mom fell in love? I mean, do you think your dad was her choice? Or was she forced into marrying him?"

"I try never to think about my parents in that way at all."

"You mean as real people?" I turn to look at her. I try to lead her very carefully. I want her to tell her mother about Cameron. Replaying today may only put off her leap in front of a train to a later moment.

She raises her eyebrows at me and screws up her mouth.

"Well, just think about it. If you talk to her about what you want to do with your life—say, going to university, seeing boys you like along the way—maybe, depending on how she sees her own life, she'll be willing to compromise."

"Yeah, but what about Dad?"

"I don't know, Jazz. My mom's definitely the boss of my father."

"I just don't want to be shipped off any earlier than this summer."

"Talk to your mother. You know you're taking a chance, anyway. Lying and hiding this thing with Cameron. It's only a matter of time."

"You don't want to cover for me anymore," Jazz says sadly.

"No! I mean, that's not it." I take her hands in mine. "You're my best friend, and I don't want you to be forced into any kind of marriage, ever."

We make it safely by the overpass to our corner. "Be careful, Jazz. Hurry home. Message me when you get there!" I walk the rest of the way to my house alone. Then I go on the computer, but of course Max hasn't put any

photos on Facebook this time. Instead, I get a message
from him.

Do you want to go out?

My heart does a quick hip-hop. I know this doesn't mean
"go out" as in go to a movie or a restaurant or anything at all
right this minute. He means, as in see each other as boyfriend and girlfriend, officially.

If I say no, it may cause the end of our friendship. If I say
yes, I will be going out with the geek of the century. Me,
Paige Barta, second-biggest geek of the century. I smile.
He'll be good-looking someday, but I can't wait. I type him
a one-word message. Yes.

That means, for the rest of my four-day life, I will be in
a relationship with Max. Better than being all alone.

Dad comes home, and this time I tell him straight out
that I want my organs donated should anything ever happen to me.

He can't even talk after that so I just stand beside him,
handing him the chili powder, cumin and cinnamon before
he asks for it. Technically this should cause Kim's elders to
zap me back to the beach, but I don't care. At least I did what
I could to save Jasmine from jumping in front of that train.

When Mom comes home, I don't have to ask her about
why Kim's parents wanted donations to the Kidney
Foundation. Instead, I follow her to her bedroom.

"Mom, do we have any pictures of me and Kim together? I seem to remember you always taking them."

She gives me one of her electric glances, sharp and questioning. "Sure, hon. Just let me get changed."

I watch as she puts her Mother's Day handprint T-shirt on. The lime color has faded. I wish I'd given her another top in these last three years. Maybe I could have tie-dyed one. My hands are so much bigger now. Then she goes into her closet and reaches up high for a heart-shaped box.

She hands it to me and I sit down on the edge of the bed, her heart on my lap. I lift the lid and pull out a book with a large square photo in the center of the cover. A serious-looking toddler with a pouty mouth and dark brown saucer eyes. *Paige's Book,* the words across it read.

"There are lots more on the CDs in Dad's boxes. Those are just the best ones I put together to have something instant to look at. A memory book."

"But then you hid it away." I flip the cover. There is one of Kim and me, each holding a silver, mouse-shaped balloon by a string in one hand. Our other hands are joined. "Second Gotcha Day," the caption reads. There are some of us at Disney World and Canada's Wonderland. "Vacation."

"We found the memories too painful. We thought they would be for you, too."

In another photo, Kim and I sit poring over a picture book. In the next photo, we must have been about five years old, hand in hand, wearing kilts and red sweaters.

"After-kindergarten playdate," it reads. We lived on oppo-
site sides of Burlington, so unfortunately didn't go to the
same school.

The shot of us both in our ladybug bathing suits sucks
the breath out of my body. We aren't toddlers in it; we must
have been close to seven years old then.

"Mom, we look so much alike."

"Yes." Mom isn't looking at me when she answers.
Something is wrong.

Next shot Kim and I are sitting on a beach digging a hole
for China, hoping to find our "real" parents. "Mom, we aren't
just a couple of babies that happen to look alike. We look
exactly the same."

"The similarity is uncanny." She nods. "Beverly Ellis and
I met at a Red Thread gathering. You and Kim found each
other immediately and started playing together."

"Red Thread," I repeat. But I already know this part of
the story.

"It was the support group for Chinese adoption families.
Once we found Bev and Kim, we didn't need anyone else.
We dropped out." Mom smiles.

"And we even came from the same orphanage and everything." Something is nagging at me, a detail I need to fully
form in my brain.

Mom nods. "We only realized that after we met."

I frown and look at the other photographs.

In the last one, we wear party hats and blow at seven

candles on a cake. "Happy seventh Gotcha Day," it reads.

Only it can't have been happy because Kim became infected with *E. coli* at that celebration. The detail finally shapes itself in my thoughts.

"Mom, we're sisters, aren't we?"

"Yes." She turns to me, her eyes shining. "Neither family knew that when we adopted you."

"But even sisters don't look that much alike." I pause, rubbing at my eyes. "We're identical."

Mom stays quiet for a few more heartbeats. "We had your DNA tested."

"Kim and I are twins?" I ask it as a question, but in my heart I know the answer.

Mom nods. "But we didn't realize that till after we met at the Red Thread meeting. You two were given to us independently. Had they kept you together as twins, neither of us would have qualified to adopt you."

"But you never told us."

"Because we couldn't raise you as sisters. We did the next best thing."

"Vacations and playdates together." I shake my head, feeling cheated. "Mom, why wouldn't you let me visit my own sister in the hospital?"

"I . . . we couldn't." Mom brushes her fingers down my hair.

"Why not?" I can feel a fist squeezing my heart. I just know the answer will be really hard to take.

"Because . . . because Bev wanted to try for a kidney transplant."

I drop my head to my hands. "And I would have been the perfect match."

"Yes." Mom circles me with her arms, and we stay that way for a few minutes while I cry. She cries, too, but finally she pulls away and speaks. "She was so weak. Giving up one of your kidneys might not have saved Kim."

"I would have liked to try."

"You have the same DNA. You could have been ill from the next hamburger."

"But we stopped eating meat."

"It doesn't need to be a hamburger. It could be a bad case of strep throat. You'd have extra risks if you ever became pregnant. You'd have to live your whole life differently if you had only one kidney."

"I would have done it for my sister."

"It wasn't your choice to make. You were too young. And we couldn't make it for you, either. The doctors wouldn't allow it."

"All these years, I thought my best friend had just left me. Now I know I was the one who abandoned her."

"Bev couldn't have us around. She didn't want to see us after. Look at me, Paige."

I raise my eyes to hers.

"She would have done the same had you been the one with the infection."

I shake my head. "It doesn't matter!" But I find I can't cry anymore. "Mom, I already told Dad, but I need you to know, too. If something happens to me, I want you to donate all my organs." *Don't hold on to a brain-dead body forever*, I silently plead. I can't tell her that out loud; I can only hope the organ donation idea will take her to the right decision.

She nods, tears sliding silently down her cheeks.

It's my turn to hug and comfort her, but I just can't. I'm still mad at her. For not helping me fight to keep Kim alive, for not taking me to see her and for hiding it all. In a couple of days, at best, I won't see my mother for a long, long time. I'll have Kim again and we'll be sisters forever. For that reason, I should be able to let the past go. I lift one hand for a moment and touch her shoulder. Then I drop it again. I just can't take that first step and forgive her.

Friday Morning

∞

Snowflakes swirl lazily outside the window the third time through Friday morning. It's funny to watch my parents struggle to come to the same decisions as they did the other two times through. I almost want to tell them what they will eventually decide. "With a storm on the way, it's not worth the risk of driving all the way to the food terminal. Go with Mom to the store instead. That way if the snow continues and no one comes in to shop, you can both come home early."

Instead, I let them come to their same conclusions. I love them even more, watching them weigh their choices. They're careful, considerate people. They don't want to let their Friday customers down. I hug Dad hard and long and then Mom, more quickly, and we all head out. The weather continues the same as the last pass through, gentle snow and warm air, not a storm by our standards.

Jasmine is late for our corner meet, so I walk to her house.

When she opens her door, instead of waiting by it and enjoying the exotic atmosphere from a distance, I kick off my boots and step into the house. "Good morning, Mrs. Aggarwal," I call. "Mmm, it smells so delicious in here."

She smiles at me broadly, a hint of Jasmine's cheekbones in the roundness of her face. "Would you like to try the *paratha* your best friend made last night?"

"Yes, please!"

She holds out a plate and I take one.

"She's been telling me that you've been teaching her to make bread." I bite into it, savoring the spicy flat dough. "It's really good," I tell Jazz.

"Ah!" Mrs. Aggarwal throws up her hands. "They look like dog's ears. She will never make a very good wife."

"But she'll make a great doctor. Did she tell you about visiting Body Worlds yesterday?"

"Yes, but you girls do not want to cut up bodies like that," she scolds.

"No. Jazz will heal people. And I will look for cures. We have it all planned out."

Mrs. Aggarwal likes that and offers me another *paratha* to take with me for lunch.

"Did she tell you she got the best mark in the class on her biology test?" I ask.

Mrs. Aggarwal turns her head to her daughter.

"She didn't, did she? She's too modest. I bet she'll beat me to all the scholarships." *If you let her continue school.* I only hope Mrs. Aggarwal will come to that same conclusion.

She offers me another *paratha*. "You need to eat more. You are too skinny. You won't find a suitable husband, either."

"Mom! Don't talk like that!"

"And who are you to be telling your own mother how to speak? The mouth on you! Doesn't matter who I send you to, they will be sending you back."

Jazz makes the silent scream face at me before she picks up her backpack from the floor in the hall.

On impulse, I hug her mother. "Thanks for the *paratha*."

She pats my back and smiles. "You are coming to the party tomorrow. Yes?"

I nod.

"There you will taste some of Beena's *pakoras*. Lured Gurindar all the way from Mumbai. Very, very good." She hugs Jasmine next, and I feel a pang. They look like each other—same warm brown skin and glowing green eyes—and they will have a lifetime of arguing and teasing together. If only Jasmine can get her to accept Cameron.

Her mother walks us to the door.

"Don't forget, I'll be home late. Paige and I are helping Mrs. Falkner in the library today."

I stop just before she shuts the door. "Mrs. Aggarwal, could we bring a couple of friends to the party?"

She looks puzzled.

"I'm sorry. That's rude, isn't it?"

"Perfectly all right. You can't be knowing any better unless your parents teach you."

"It's only because we're studying India in school and they'll never get to know the real culture, not from a book and a class."

Her mother nods. "Most certainly you should bring them. More people will bring Gurindar and Beena good luck."

"Thank you. Bye."

Her mother waves from the window as we walk away, down the sidewalk toward school.

At the end of the block, I look back, but she isn't watching us anymore. It's strange how some small details change each time I live through different parts of this week.

"What was that about?" Jazz asks in a frazzle. "Who are you bringing?"

"Who do you think?"

"Are you crazy?"

"You didn't talk to her about Cameron, did you?" I ask.

"A little. I didn't come out and tell her about him. But I said I might like to choose my own husband."

"What did she say?"

"She said it was too early for any of that. As long as I was a good girl, we would just go to India for a visit. Didn't matter what my grandfather and Dad cooked up."

"Well, that's great news."

"I'm not a good girl. At least, not the way she thinks." Jasmine sighs and shakes her head. "Well, okay, let's see how Cameron does with my family at the *sagai*." She stoops down and picks up some snow to form into a snowball. "I can decide how to tell them about him after." She pitches the snowball high in the air and hits a pole. "Thanks for everything."

"No problem." I throw a snowball, too, but it misses and lands on the ground. Ahead I see Max and Vanessa talking together. Of all people. As we walk closer, I can hear their conversation.

"You should try a nicotine patch, worked for my father," he tells her.

She scowls.

He runs up to me then. "Can I carry your backpack?"

I shake my head. "You can knock it off, is what you can do."

He leans over and kisses my cheek. "We're going out together," he tells Jasmine. "Did she tell you that?"

"Not yet," I answer, then turn to Jazz. "It's true, I'm afraid."

Her eyes look like they've jumped into her eyebrows.

I grin at her reaction.

"Great! Good." She recovers almost instantly and pats my arm.

Of the three walks to school, this one has definitely turned out the best.

Till Vanessa walks toward us and shoves Jasmine backward. "You better stay away from Cameron."

"Hey, hey," Max calls out and quickly steps between

them. Both Vanessa and Jasmine tower over him. He looks a little silly, like a mouse between two warring giraffes.

Jasmine steps around Max and comes back for more. "I would, really, Vanessa. To help you out, I mean. Only it's Cameron who can't stay away from me." Jazz doesn't wait for Vanessa's mouth to close again. Instead, she barrels past her, throwing her to one side this time. Max and I follow.

"When I finish with you, Brownie," Vanessa calls after her, "he'll find it pretty easy. Trust me."

I wince, wondering what she has in mind. Breaking Jazz's nose or slashing her face.

"This is too much," Max says as we continue into the school. "We both heard her threaten you, Jasmine. We need to report her."

"Yeah," I agree. Something has changed about Max. I watch him as he holds the door open for us. He seems to have more confidence, to be more courageous somehow. I shake my head. "Did you have to goad her quite so much, Jazz? You know she'll have her whole army after you now."

"Oh, she would have anyway, even if I had stayed quiet." She lowers her voice as we walk to our lockers. "I'm not dropping Cameron because of her threats. She's going to get that through her head sooner or later."

"Yeah, well, it might not be soon enough." I lower my voice, too. "What do you think, Jazz? If we tell Mrs. Norr, Vanessa will get suspended."

"And that will leave the rest of the volleyball team."

"Maybe without their leader, they won't be so keen," Max suggests.

He's right. How can we just do nothing? But then another thought occurs to me. "If Jasmine has a threat made against her, and Mrs. Norr knows, will she call in all the parents?" I ask the question but know the answer.

"I think so."

"Mine, too?" Jazz squeaks. "I can't have Mom or Dad involved."

"Probably," Max answers. "Who knows?"

Of course, I know because of the Body Worlds photo of the intertwined cadaver couple, the one with Jazz's and Cameron's heads Photoshopped on top. But that event hasn't really happened, since I backtracked a day again.

"Promise me you won't say anything about it to her, then. Both of you. I can't have my parents know."

Max shrugs his shoulders.

I sigh. "Whatever." If she told her parents about Cameron, maybe this could turn out differently.

Cameron joins us then, and we leave Jazz and him alone while we go off to science together.

The topic of discussion today, of course, is Body Worlds. Mr. Brewster tells us the various other ways cadavers are used to help science. I always thought they used dummies for crash tests, but he tells us real cadavers are needed for seat-belt testing and air-bag impact. "Statistics show that every body donated saves a hundred and forty-seven lives. And that's just with bodies, not organs."

I don't want my body to be used for safety testing, but I really want my kidneys to save a couple of kids. That will make up for not being able to help Kim. If my heart and lungs work out for someone else, or if my eyes can let someone see, that will be a bonus.

In English, Shakespeare is really growing on me. Max and I are teamed up to translate a love scene into modern English. His job is to read the passage out loud, and then we both work on interpreting. I write it down. I watch Max's face, seeing his wide nose and lips differently today. He reads flat, in a matter-of-fact tone that makes Romeo's overblown love confession funny.

"Oh baby, oh baby, oh baby," I say as I paraphrase his lines.

He laughs and I find myself not minding his square bangs anymore. Spending time with Max is like reading Shakespeare, an acquired taste. I'm going to miss him.

To cheer myself up, I think about spending time with Kim. Since I will never know who my real parents are, I'm glad to find that I have one real biological relation, my sister. And we can explore all eternity together.

"Let's go outside," I tell Max at first break. "I don't want to get in the path of the volleyball team."

"And give up my hamburger fix?" he protests.

"I've got some Indian food I can share with you. Jazz's mom gave it to me." I tuck my arm in his elbow on the way to the locker. After we put on our coats, we head outside. I see them before they spot me, so I steer Max away from the football field.

"They're all out there smoking," Max says. "How long before they get kicked off the team?"

"We won't have any team."

"Maybe they'll go into rehab." Max grins as we walk across the street. We find our way to a park bench a few blocks away from the school.

There I split up the *paratha*.

"I love Indian food more than hamburger and pizza combined," Max tells me.

"Good, then you'll like coming to Beena's engagement party on Saturday. She makes great *pakoras*."

"What? I don't know Beena."

"She's Jasmine's cousin."

"Do I need to bring a present?"

"I don't know. We'll ask Jazz later. Isn't this good? Can you believe Jazz made this?"

"Wow. She makes bread from scratch?"

I nod. "She's being trained to cook Indian food so she'll make a good wife, just like Beena."

"Well, she makes a mean *paratha*."

Then I explain to him exactly why Jazz doesn't want her parents called in about the bullying. "If they hear about Cameron before Jazz can explain, she thinks they'll take her to India immediately to find a husband."

"What is there to explain? Indian girls aren't supposed to date at all, are they?"

"No. But Jazz's parents came to the West for a reason. They must want more opportunity for their kids. Cameron's coming to the party, too. He doesn't know it yet, but he is."

"You're kidding. Paige, this could so backfire."

"We have to try something. This way there's a chance the Aggarwals will get to know him before they find out Jazz is seeing him."

"Vanessa would sure tell them if she knew it would cause trouble." Max pauses a moment as though thinking something over. "You know, if Mrs. Norr found out about those girls smoking on school property, they would be suspended, too."

"She'd call in their parents but not Jazz's. I like that idea! How would we prove it?"

"Come on. If they're still out there, maybe we can catch them in the act." Max and I run back to school. It isn't snowing now, not even a flake, and the volleyball team still stands around at the far edge of the football field, cigarettes in hand.

"How close do you plan on getting?" I ask Max.

"Pretty close. No zoom on my cell phone. We better run fast after."

I'm fed up with running already. Finally, we're close enough for Max to hold out his cell and click! And another just to make sure he has a good clear image.

"What are you doing?" Vanessa yells. "Get that phone off him!" She points and Kierstead, Emma and Morgan run after us.

"Too bad. I've already e-mailed it to myself," Max calls back.

We run directly for the front door, up the stairs and into the office. "Could we speak to Mrs. Norr?" I ask the secretary.

"What is it?" Mrs. Norr calls as she steps out from behind her desk. "Come in," she adds.

"Isn't it against the law for anyone to smoke on school property?" Max asks as we enter her office.

"You know it is. We told everyone in assembly earlier this month," she answers.

We line up side by side in front of her desk. "Well, there are some students who routinely go to the edge of the football field and smoke at break."

"Did you want to tell me their names?" She looks at us skeptically.

We're tattling, squealing, snitching, all those things that break the unwritten code of honor. But I know what Vanessa is capable of, and if we can just do something to keep her away from Jasmine for this one day, so she can talk about Cameron with her folks, maybe all of destiny can change. This time in a good way.

Friday Afternoon

∞

M rs. Norr squints at the tiny screen as Max holds it up toward her.

"You don't have to believe us or even the cell phone," Max says. "Just call them all in and smell for yourself."

Mrs. Norr's mouth tugs downward. "But I can't control their smoking altogether. And the smell doesn't prove they've been doing it on school property."

I don't understand her stalling. "You can make out the goalpost in that shot. See that white thing behind Vanessa McDonald's head?"

Mrs. Norr nods, steepling her fingers. "I'm wondering why you two are stepping forward to report these girls."

"Vanessa was really upset about the black lung we saw at Body Worlds yesterday," Max says.

"You can ask Mr. Brewster," I add. "I know her mother smokes, too."

"Yes, her mother might be Vanessa's biggest problem." Mrs. Norr taps her fingers together, still delaying.

"I think if she got in trouble for it, she might just be convinced to quit," Max says.

"Well, that's very noble of you both." Mrs. Norr opens her fingers again and places her palms down on the desk as though finally ready to push off. Only she hesitates. "Is there something else going on that you want to tell me about?"

I look at Max and he looks back at me. The bullying. I sigh. I'm sick and tired of suffering the shoves and insults from that stupid volleyball gang. But we promised Jazz we wouldn't say anything about Vanessa's threats so I button my lip. "No, Mrs. Norr," we both answer.

"Very well. Leave your phone with me for this period, Max. You may go."

We dash out. It doesn't take long for the announcement. "Would the following students report to the office immediately: Vanessa McDonald, Kierstead Compo, Morgan Pellam, Laura Gingham, Gwyn Thompson, Emma Simmons, Zoe O'Connell and Rebecca Bennett." I feel revenge smirk inside me. That's what you get for posting photos of naked corpses with my best friend's and her boyfriend's heads on them.

Only they haven't done that this lifetime through.

I pass Emma and Zoe in the hall as I head for gym class. They look at each other, then glare at me. Zoe taps her nose as she raises an eyebrow.

Oh, big threat! As fast as their parents are called and letters are written, they're going to have to leave the school premises. If they want to meet us at the overpass to beat us up, at the very least they will be seriously inconvenienced. Maybe their parents will ground them. Or maybe they will be leery of getting into any more trouble and risking expulsion.

In any case, gym class is never quite as relaxed as today. No one slams me into a locker or knocks me with any equipment. We play volleyball without the pros, and I actually get a serve across. No one double blocks or spikes it back. No one squabbles with each other over missing the shots or serves or calling for the ball. My side wins by a few points, but it doesn't even matter. Everyone seems to have fun, and no one snaps a wet towel at me in the changing room.

In French class, the drills go quicker, and Madame Potvin gives out e-mail addresses for possible pen pals for us. She also talks about the exchange trip she's arranging for spring break.

If only there was some way I could avoid that train Monday afternoon, I would see Paris. I smile, imagining the Eiffel Tower. But the deal was a week to return so that I could stand up for Jazz this time, and I have to keep my side of the bargain. Still, hasn't so much else changed because I acted on some of my better impulses? If only I hadn't spent my lifetime behind that shell I'd created. Who knows how much better everything would have gone?

On the way to the library at the end of the day, I make the mistake of stopping at my locker. Someone has smeared something red and meaty across it. Spaghetti sauce?

"I've got it! No worries," Max calls as he runs my way. He carries a spray bottle in one hand and a plastic bag and rag in another. "I had way more on my locker. Whoever cooked it likes their meat rare." He immediately begins wiping the red stuff into the bag.

"Thanks, Max. I'm so glad I'm not alone in this."

He stops mid-wipe, suddenly looking a little green.

"What's wrong?"

"I think I just wiped off an eyeball."

"Oh my gawd. What is this really?" I step in closer.

Max's neck stretches out and his shoulders lift, like he's ready to hurl.

I step back.

"My guess is roadkill, squirrel probably." He looks away for a minute, taking a couple of breaths. Then he quickly finishes.

"You don't think we should report any of this?" I ask.

"What more can Mrs. Norr do today? They're already suspended. Not even supposed to be on school property."

I shake my head. Those girls found plastinated body parts gross, so smearing squirrel on our lockers shows real dedication on their part. "Do you want to try to catch up to Jazz and Cameron?" I ask Max. "Warn them? Maybe they should go home early. On the bus, preferably."

"Sure." He gives the locker a couple more swipes as I throw on my coat for the trek to find Jazz and Cameron.

"Hurry," I tell Max as I move ahead of him through the

hall and out the back of the school. I try to run, lifting my feet high over the duvet of snow spread across the field. It's exhausting. On the sidewalk it becomes easier, although by this time I'm out of breath. "Down this block, this is the way they always go." I point and we turn.

At the end of the street, I think I see them. At least, it's two people huddled together, walking. "Jasmine! Cameron!"

They turn and she waves.

"Hold up a minute!" I call. I sigh as we head closer. Whatever happens, at least there will be four of us together. Then I have a second thought. Last time, both Jazz and I got hit by the train. What if all four of us are killed this pass? "Max, I don't feel like rushing home right now. If we hang out at the mall awhile, one of my parents could drive us."

"Let's see how Jazz reacts when you tell her about the roadkill," he answers.

"What's Max talking about?" Jazz asks as we draw closer.

"How was your locker today?"

"Fine. Vanessa and her gang were sent home, remember?"

"Still, one of them managed to splatter squirrel on our lockers."

"Gross!" Jazz says.

"That can't be Vanessa. She faints at the sight of blood," Cameron says.

"Doesn't matter which one of them did it. I think we should stick together. Safety in numbers," I suggest.

"I'm not afraid of Vanessa," Cameron answers.

"You probably don't need to be," I say. "But what about Jazz?"

"Why don't we go to the mall with you?" Max asks. "You may want to pick out an engagement present, anyway."

"What are you talking about?" Cameron asks as we start walking in that direction. Max and I squeeze in together beside Cameron and Jazz.

Jazz answers, her face pink. "Paige got you and Max invited to my cousin's engagement party on Saturday."

"Great. I get to see you," Cameron says.

Last time through the weekend, I had to cover for them when they went to a movie.

"Yeah, well, you can't touch me or act like a boyfriend in any way," Jazz warns. "Don't worry about buying a present, though. Indians only give money."

"A card, then," I suggest. "We want Cameron to make a good impression."

We cross the parking lot to the mall now. "Plus, I could use something to wear. You can help me buy something that's . . . appropriate."

Cameron holds open the first door for us, and instantly warm air rushes around us. We stamp our feet on the rubber mat. Max gets the second door. "Let's grab a hot chocolate first," Max suggests, and we head for the food court. The mall is pretty empty at this hour. A girl steps forward to try to get us to sample her special Dead Sea salt scrub, but we dart around her.

"You don't have to buy anything to wear," Jazz tells me. "I'll lend you a sari."

"Okay, I'd like that." Probably the closest I'll ever get to travel to the East.

The smell of coffee and vanilla leads us to the doughnut shop. At a table nearby, I notice someone hunched over an empty cup and crumpled napkin. I nudge Max, but Cameron has already spotted her. She doesn't look scary here all alone. She looks washed-out and sad.

Cameron turns to Jazz. "She hangs out here whenever she has a fight with her mom. Do you mind? I have to go check on her."

We watch as Cameron walks over to her. I see how Vanessa wipes at tears and mucus as she sobs. Pathetic. Not a look to get a guy back. I can't really hear what they say to each other.

Cameron shrugs his shoulders and takes out his wallet. He leaves a few bills on the table for Vanessa, then returns to us.

"Is she okay?" Jasmine asks.

"She's kicked out of the house again. Her mother's mad about her smoking suspension."

"Oh gawd. Why doesn't she sleep over at a friend's?" I ask. "It's cold out. She can't stay at the mall forever."

"Most of them are grounded, too. And I know my parents are fed up with her crashing in our basement."

I stare after Vanessa. Her head is buried in her hands, and her hair sticks out like feathers. She's lost her boyfriend, who was maybe her best friend, too. No place to stay in February. I shake my head.

"Let's go get the card," Jazz suggests. "I can't sit here with her across from me, looking like that."

"All right. Where to?" Cameron asks. He sounds as dragged down as I feel.

"Over there." I point to a gift shop. We walk into it and start browsing. The clerk has to show us where the engagement cards are since there are only four to choose from: A cutesy red heart card that says, "U've got hitched"; another with a pair of gold bands that reads, "To the best couple ever"; and another with a big diamond on a girl's hand: "You've found your Mr. Right."

The final card, "You have found your soul mate," I pick for myself.

"Oh man, they're five bucks! I gave all my money to Van just now," Cameron says. "Can I just sign yours, Jazz?"

"No, we can't be linked!" Jazz says. "Pitch in with Max. Here, I'll lend you ten."

"That's okay, I've got money," Max says.

"I've still got some change," Cameron says.

"Whatever. Make it an uneven amount, like eleven," Jazz suggests. "The extra dollar is considered lucky."

"Good, we can stop shopping," Max says. "I'll design a better card at home."

As I reach in my backpack to pay for the one I chose, we hear a commotion from the food court. A voice is swearing. A raspy female voice.

In another minute, we see two security guards dragging Vanessa to the door. She isn't putting up that much of a struggle—just cursing loudly.

Revenge doesn't feel all that sweet; it feels uncomfortable, a heavy guilty lump. Will Van really have no place to go because we reported her smoking on school property? Max and I look at each other.

"She'll go to the library next," Cameron says. "Hang out there till Kierstead texts her back."

"Kierstead?" I repeat.

"She didn't get suspended. Apparently she never smoked. All the other girls vouched for her with Mrs. Norr."

"I didn't see her in French class, though," I say.

"Well, maybe she skipped."

"So she could smear squirrel guts on our lockers," Max grumbles.

She'll be the one to plan the ambush, then, I think. We should be safe till Monday, at least. Alone, Vanessa isn't going to beat up anyone.

"How about that hot chocolate now?" Max suggests.

The mood is spoiled for me. Feeling sorry for my worst enemy—and yet scared of her, too—does that to me. Still, it's too early to call my parents for a lift, and I don't want to hit the cold again, either.

"Come on," Max repeats, draping his arm around me. He has to reach up to get it over my shoulder, but he doesn't seem to mind.

Jazz smiles and shakes her head. Max seems so proud to go out with me, I have to get over myself.

We end up having a good time, too. Jazz does impersonations of her mother to prepare us. "They always give you their opinions straight out; you never have to ask," she complains and then puts on an Indian accent and wags her finger. "Why is it that you are so short, Max? You need to put inserts in your shoes when you are going out with such a beanpole girl."

I laugh.

"And what are you laughing at? Take some more *paratha*. Your boyfriend will need something to hold on to when he climbs up to kiss you." She pats Cameron's shoulder. "You seem like a very nice boy. You should find yourself some equally nice *gora* to fool around with, eh?"

Cameron smiles and shrugs. "You're the only one for me." He reaches over and stops her with a kiss.

A sweet moment. He can't help himself.

Neither can Max. He pretends to climb up on the seat so he can reach me to kiss. I laugh. The hot chocolate tastes good after that, and when I call Foods R Good on my cell, Dad picks up and says he and Mom are just leaving. With the van, they have room to drive all of us home.

Saturday — The Engagement Party

∞

Next day, I head over to Jasmine's house with my card that now holds my last twenty-one dollars of allowance in it. After Monday, I probably won't be needing any money, anyway. Jazz points me to the slotted box on the carved elephant table near the front, and I drop it in. Then she takes me into her room. On the bed lies a long, wide, turquoise scarf with delicate pink flowers along the edge. "That's your sari. But this goes under first." She hands me a plain white skirt. "And here's a top." Jazz flings a pink halter at me.

I put them both on.

"Great. Now let me help you with this." She wraps the turquoise fabric around me. "Flowered border to the bottom. Tuck this into the slip." I do as she asks, and she helps me adjust it so the fabric touches the ground. Then she brings it around and folds it into five pleats and I tuck those in. Around and over my shoulder.

"Wow." I look at myself in the mirror. "But so much of my stomach shows. Is that all right?"

She puts on her accent again. "You are a pretty young girl. It is perfectly acceptable." She wags her finger. She drops the accent. "Legs not so much."

"Won't it fall apart if we dance wildly?"

"No question of *if.* We *will* dance wildly. Here." She hands me a safety pin. "Tack your shoulder down. Your sari will *never* come off."

The doorbell rings then and Mrs. Aggarwal calls out, "Paige, your friends have arrived."

Jazz rolls her eyes and sighs, "Here goes!"

We swish to the front door in time to see Max hand Mrs. Aggarwal a covered cake dish. "Dessert," Max grins. "Profiteroles. My dad helped me make them."

"You are worried that Indians do not know how to make dessert?"

"No, not at all!" Max's eyes pop.

Mrs. Aggarwal winks. "Just kidding." She lifts the lid. There sits a pyramid of puffs with white cream centers and chocolate sauce drooling over. "Ah, you made *gulab jamun*! Wonderful."

"They're profiteroles."

She waves her hand. "Chinese *gulab jamun*. Will bring good luck."

Jasmine winces. "They're French, Mom, not Chinese. Pastry. Hard to make."

"But he made them, not his mother." Mrs. Aggarwal seems confused.

"My father works as a chef, and he helped," Max explains.

"Ah."

"We brought a card," Cameron says shyly.

"Can I see first?" I ask.

"This is most rude, no?" Mrs. Aggarwal asks.

"But they designed it themselves, and they're very proud," I answer her, and she leans over my shoulder to look, too. I untuck the flap carefully and slide it out. On the outside, within a golden heart, an Indian guy in a white suit looks soulfully at a gorgeous girl in a red sari. On the inside it says, "For Beena and Gurindar. The most precious treasure in the world cannot be seen or touched, it must be felt within the heart."

Mrs. Aggarwal claps her hands. "Oh, that is beautiful. Not very much money," she says, noticing the eleven dollars enclosed, "but beautiful words. Put it in the box and go have something to eat."

"I read it in a fortune cookie," Max whispers to me as Cameron takes it back and slips it into the slot.

We head through the dining room and kitchen, sampling appetizers that make my breath feel like dragon's fire. *Pakoras, samosas* and *chaat papri*, different aunts explain, all insisting I must eat more, I really am too skinny. Everything seems vaguely like a deep-fried dough pocket of spices and vegetables. Mostly spices.

Max and Cameron enjoy it all. We finally wind our way to the family room, where the ceremony is about to take place.

Beena and Gurindar sit together. Once everyone gathers around, Beena's father leans over Gurindar and with his finger traces a circle on his forehead, a third eye *chakra*, Jazz explains. Then he hands him a coconut with a gold bracelet inside. Gurindar's dad makes the same circle on Beena's forehead. Then the fathers and mothers feed the couple little sweets. Finally, Gurindar slips a diamond ring on Beena's finger.

Relatives begin congratulating them and handing them money.

"Isn't he going to kiss her?" I whisper to Jazz.

"Are you kidding? That's too much like sex for Indians."

Not as romantic as I would like. Still, everyone seems so happy. I lean over to Jazz. "You don't want this, too?"

Jazz shrugs her shoulders.

From the other corner of the family room, a sound system suddenly begins pumping out Indian music, and men and women jump up. Max and I stand and swirl to the music, too, hands raised high in the air.

Jazz yanks me away from him and gives me a warning glare. Now it looks as though Max and Cameron are dancing together. No one could guess Jazz and Cameron are a couple. Wilder and louder we whirl and swirl, till at one point someone steps on my sari and I can feel my dress dragging off me.

"Ahh!" I yelp and yank it out from under a man's foot.

He bows his head in apology, and I quickly duck into the powder room. Jazz follows me. She laughs as she rewinds the turquoise fabric around me. "I've never heard of anyone's sari coming off. You're a first." This time she pins the shoulder down.

Mrs. Aggarwal sees us come out. "Why don't you wear a kimono? We are very multicultural here in Canada."

"Mom! Paige is Chinese not Japanese."

"You know what I mean. The satin dress, the clingy one that looks like a Nehru jacket."

I chuckle. "A *cheongsam*. I don't own one. I'm adopted."

"Still. Your Canadian mother should buy you one."

My Canadian mother, I chew my lip, *already owns one herself*. It's only me who finds Chinese culture so appalling. "Are you really multicultural, Mrs. Aggarwal? Does anyone ever marry a *gora*?" I use Jazz's word for a white person.

Beside me, Jazz's eyes look like they will pop from her face.

"Oh, most certainly. My cousin Baljeet married a French Canadian girl. Big embarrassment to his family. She does make the best goat curry, though."

"Good curry is important, right?" I smile. "No girls marrying non-Indian boys?"

Jazz kicks me.

"Not yet. You know it's just easier when like marries like."

"It might be easier," I agree. "But how do you meet someone like yourself . . ." *when you're a Chinese orphan with*

Caucasian parents? Plus the Chinese rarely give up boys for adoption unless they're mentally or physically challenged. The music starts up again, so she doesn't hear the end of my question and we can't finish the discussion. Okay, I can see it isn't going to be easy for Jazz, but still she should see there is hope.

We dance again and, despite a night that continues wild and joyful, no other saris fall apart.

I want more of that joy. Monday can't be the end of this for me. Does it have to be? Can I help Jazz and help myself stay alive, too?

Max and Cameron leave at midnight, but since I'm sleeping over, I get to stay till the very end and carry dishes of leftovers to the kitchen.

We help ourselves to some of Max's delicious profiteroles as we put away the food.

"Really, they are very nice boys," Mrs. Aggarwal tells us. "It is too bad they are gay."

I sputter out cream puff.

"What?" Jazz asks.

"They made such nice poetry together, and they baked these lovely French *gulab jamun*. But didn't you notice, they only danced with each other?"

Jazz and I snicker.

"I agree. They really are very nice boys," Jazz says.

We don't even try to change her mother's mind. It may be to Jazz's advantage, anyway.

Sunday Afternoon

∞

We wake up just before noon. I rub at my gritty eyes and listen to Jazz complain about her family, how prejudiced they are. "Francine goes out of her way to be more Indian than the rest of them, and still she's an embarrassment."

"But they're so much fun. You'd never catch my mom or dad dancing like that."

"Yeah. And Cameron's gay 'cause he didn't dance with a girl. If he'd danced with anyone but you, they would have had a cow."

I chuckle. "You have family." I pause. "I found out this week Kim was my sister."

"What! Oh my gawd, Paige!"

"She never moved away, either. She died of an *E. coli* infection."

"So you found some real biological family and lost it at the same time?"

I nod. "It gets worse. We were identical twins. Our parents must have separated us and dumped us at different lampposts."

"And here I am complaining about my parents. Sorry."

"Don't be. But you can see why I don't want to get into my Chinese heritage."

"What about Kim's parents? I mean, the adoptive ones. Have you ever visited them? Imagine, they could actually see what their daughter might have grown up to be."

"I never thought of them." I feel my face get warm. What did Kim say about me when I last saw her? *It's always about you.* When Dad tensed up over organ transplants, Mom told me *to think about someone else's feelings for a change.* The shell I hid behind gave me distance, but it also cut me off. "Seeing me could go two ways, too, you know," I continue. "I mean, wouldn't it hurt too much?"

"Well, you could call first."

"True." *But I only have half of today and Monday left in my life.* I have to make a quick decision. "Jazz, can you let me browse your computer for her telephone number?"

"Wow, the engagement party really had an effect on you."

"Maybe," I answer.

She takes me to the kitchen, where the family computer sits in an alcove. Finding the phone number is easy. There are three Ellises in the database but only one on Longsmoor Drive. But should I really call them? If I can't change destiny, they will meet me today and tomorrow hear about my accident. Another loss for them. During this last week, when I finally stepped out from my shell, incredible things happened. Now when I try to understand how others might feel, it becomes too hard.

I borrow the Aggarwal phone. Step one, I have to at least try to reconnect.

The phone rings once before Kim's mom picks up.

"Hello?"

In the one word, a flood of memories returns. She used to make crafts with Kim and me, shopped for candy to decorate a huge birthday cookie. She French-braided our hair and stuck in white baby's breath.

"Hello?" she repeats. "Who is this?"

"Aunt Bev? It's me."

"Paige." She answers in a sigh. Not with sadness but with warmth. I can hear a smile in her voice, and suddenly all I want to do is to see her and hug her and live my whole childhood through again.

"Can I come to see you?"

"Of course. Anytime."

"Today? Right now?"

"That would be wonderful."

I ask her about bus directions since their house is at the other end of the city for me. She tells me she would pick me up except that Uncle Jack is at the hardware store with their only car. When I get off the phone, Mrs. Aggarwal offers to drive me.

"Thanks," I tell her.

Jazz jumps in the back of the large black truck her family drives, just to keep me company.

Tiny Mrs. Aggarwal peers through the steering wheel as she maneuvers through the slow streets of Burlington to the southeast end.

At the small ranch house that I once knew so well, she lets me off.

"Want me to come, too?" Jazz asks.

"Thanks, but no. I'll be fine." I climb out of the truck and wave to Jazz and her mom.

Before I can knock on the door, it opens, and Kim's mom spreads her arms wide to me. "It's so good to see you."

I fall into them. Aunt Bev is a short round woman with light brown hair, blue eyes and freckles. Strands of silver glint from her hair now, less gray than Mom's, though. Wrinkles fan out from her eyes and the corners of her mouth, but she feels like bed cushions when I hug her back. I can smell vanilla and chocolate warm in the air as I step into the house.

"As soon as I got off the phone, I started baking cookies." With her arm on my shoulder, she leads me through the living room, where I can see pictures of me and Kim everywhere. So different from my house, where they are all locked away. The kitchen looks different: no rooster wallpaper; the cabinets are painted a butterscotch color. Before, I'm sure they'd been white. "Do you want milk or tea with your cookies?" she asks me as I sit down on the stool at the counter.

"Tea, please." Now I remember a tiny pink and white set of cups and saucers and little teapot that sang as Kim poured. What was that tune? Her dad used to sing along in a funny papa bear kind of voice.

Aunt Bev plugs in the kettle, then bends over to pull the cookie sheet from the oven. All this I missed. I squeeze my eyes shut tightly.

"How is your mother?" she asks as she places a plate of cookies in front of me. "Careful, they're still hot."

I lift one up anyway, and it breaks in my hands. "Mmm. She only makes carob." I bite into the melting buttery sweetness. "Mostly she brings home organic."

"But she's kept her figure after all these years." Aunt Bev smiles. "You're so beautiful." Standing next to me, she strokes my arm.

"You've seen Mom?"

"From a distance. I've always respected her space."

"I didn't even know you still lived in Burlington."

"It's what your parents thought best. I knew someday you would look for us." She pours from the kettle into a teapot now.

"But I thought you had moved to another part of the country."

"Sooner or later, you would have discovered the truth." She sits down beside me, placing the teapot on a trivet.

"I didn't know about the *E. coli*." I hesitate. "I'm so mad at Mom. I would have gladly done anything to keep Kim alive."

"It wasn't anybody's fault." Aunt Bev bites into a cookie, and I watch as her eyes turn teary. "But your mom just couldn't give up on Kimberly."

"What are you talking about? She should have insisted on a kidney transplant. Mine had to be a perfect match."

Her tears spilled over. "Kimmee was so weak, honey. I couldn't allow it."

"But Mom said . . ." I stop.

"No doctor around here would consent to a live organ transplant from such a little girl. You would have had to be at least sixteen. Your mother found a doctor in India, but we couldn't go along with it. It was too big a risk."

It makes sense. I can picture Mom at my bedside trying to get me to squeeze her hand or to blink my eyes long after everyone else has given up on me. "She should have let me visit Kim."

"Maybe. But she went so quickly, and you were very young." She hugs me. "Don't waste your time being angry."

She's right. With only Monday left, I have no more time to waste. "Do you think Mom would be ready to see you?" I ask her.

"After all these years, I hope so," Aunt Bev answers.

Maybe with some luck, they would bond again, and then when Mom needed to pull the plug and let me go, Aunt Bev would be there for her. "I have an idea," I say, "let's all go out for Chinese."

Aunt Bev likes the idea, so for my last supper together on

this earth, I call Mom at the store and tell her we should meet at the Mandarin.

"For a Canadian, Chinese, Japanese kind of smorgasbord?" she asks, laughing.

"Yes. I'm embracing my roots. Mixed as they are. Mom? Aunt Bev and Uncle Jack are coming."

There's a sharp intake of breath. "I see." Then there's a long silence. Finally, she speaks. "It's probably time. Okay, then. We're locking up now. We should be there in twenty minutes."

No argument from her, even though I put her on the spot. That was easy.

Uncle Jack arrives home as I set down the phone. "Well, look who the cat dragged in," he says in a pleased voice. He's lost most of his hair since I last saw him, and he looks shorter, if that's possible. Like Aunt Bev, he's put on weight.

"Don't get too settled. We're meeting Paige's parents for dinner."

"Really?" He looks me over slowly, his face opening like a sunrise. "Just see how beautiful our girl turned out." He smiles. "Everything we could have imagined."

It was exactly what I would have wanted my biological parents to say if I could have found them somehow. Uncle Jack and Aunt Bev instantly fill a hole; maybe it's the one Kim and I were always digging.

Uncle Jack opens his arms. I stand up and step into his bear hug.

After a few moments, Bev taps my arm. "Time to go. Let's get our coats."

Jack holds Bev's out as she slides her arms in. Then we all head out to the car in the driveway. They've replaced their larger four-door sedan with an electric blue hatchback. Kind of zippy and tiny for such slow-moving big people. I slide behind the pushed-up seat.

We beat my parents to the restaurant, so we put our names down for a table. When they finally arrive, I watch Mom hesitate and stumble over her words. "It's been so long, it's so good . . ." One hand lifts, then the other. . . .

Aunt Bev rushes to hug her. The dads shake hands and lie about how they haven't changed a bit. One set of parents looks too thin and the other too heavy. They all look a bit sad and tired. Everyone and everything has changed.

The hostess interrupts to show us to the back, a room almost to ourselves.

By this time tears shine in Mom's eyes. "We've let too much time go by."

"I wish we could have been there for you," Dad adds.

Uncle Jack shakes his head. "Seeing Paige today is just perfect."

The waiter stops by, and I ask for chopsticks. He whisks away my cutlery and lays down a package.

"I'm a little nervous about eating here," Mom says.

To say the least, I think. *How do they feel about sitting and dining with Kim's parents after everything that happened?*

"All that food sits out under hot lights for a long time," Dad agrees.

"Don't worry. This is a popular place. They replenish the dishes frequently," Jack tells them.

"Let's get up there," I suggest, and we line up behind the other diners. I take shrimp, sushi, egg rolls, a steamed dumpling and something that looks like a stuffed dead leaf. I think it might be authentic Chinese. Back at our seats, I fail several times to lift the brown leaf bundle to my mouth. Finally, I lower my face and scoop it in. Instantly, I begin choking.

My mother rubs my back. "You're not supposed to eat the lotus leaf."

It's dry and tasteless and doesn't dissolve, so I spit it into a napkin.

"The dim sum chef steams food in the leaf to give it a good color and aroma," Bev explains.

"You're supposed to hold the chopsticks more like a pencil," Mom continues.

"Okay." I drop the chopsticks with a sigh. "I've changed my mind, Mom. Let's go to China."

"Well, that's a big leap. From the buffet to another continent," Dad says.

"I always wanted to take Kim," Bev says.

"We were going to take you together; that was the plan," Mom says, frowning.

"Why don't we still do that?" I suggest. "The more the merrier." *Is there even a million-to-one chance I can avoid that train tomorrow? Avoid some other death that may replace the train accident?* Will Mom and Bev somehow stay in contact after my death? In my mind, I picture them going together despite my death.

Everyone gets along well. It's as though the tragedy of Kim's death had bonded us instead of creating that seven-year rift. Mom is going to inquire at the travel agency next to their store about a group discount for five. Bev says to call her with a time and she will meet her there with a list of must-go-to places. We start tasting foods from each other's plates. Mom accidentally eats some beef but doesn't make a fuss about it.

When the tea comes at the end, I open my fortune cookie. It says: *Destiny has other plans for you.* I shudder.

D-day Morning

∞

*T**his'll be the day that I die.* It's the line from one of my parents' favorite songs, but it's also true. I leap out of bed the moment the alarm sounds at seven, greedy to enjoy much more of the day than last time, when I buried my head under the pillow. After I dress, I head to the kitchen and pause when I see Mom staring out the window watching the sunrise.

"Good morning." Mom sips from her coffee.

I sit down beside her and look outside, too. A thin line of orange glows along the horizon.

"Why did you make me think it was Aunt Bev who wanted the kidney transplant? Why didn't you tell me it was you?"

The horizon swells with a bump of bright gold.

She turns to me. "Because I was ashamed." She sips again. "I was so wrong about it."

The bump becomes a perfect small orb, the gold spreading around it.

"How do you know? Kim could have been alive today."

She shakes her head. "Did you ever hear the story of wise King Solomon and the two mothers?"

"This is from the Bible, isn't it?" The sky transforms now. Clouds begin to light up in pink and gold.

She nods.

"When's the last time you took me to church?"

"Never, but I thought you might have studied it in school, literature or something." As she speaks, the sky continues to open into soft Popsicle pinks and purples.

I can't believe I missed this display last time.

"Anyway, two women come before King Solomon, both claiming to be the mother of the same baby boy. One of the women had accidentally killed her son by rolling over in her sleep." Mom pauses and drains her cup. "King Solomon tells his guards to cut the baby in half and give each mother a piece."

"But that would be killing him. Neither would get a live child."

"Exactly. So one steps forward and tells the king to give the whole baby to the other woman. At least he would stay alive."

"Oh, I have heard this one. So the king declares that woman the real mother because she loves him enough to save him, even if it means giving him up."

"That's right." Mom looks up at me. "So tell me, Paige, which mother was I?"

"Oh, come on. Giving away one kidney isn't like cutting a baby in half."

"Taking a severely ill child to India? Risking a healthy child?" She shakes her head. "Bev was right. This way, at least one child lived. But maybe I was the wrong mother to keep her."

"How could you even think that?"

"Because Bev made the sacrifice without even asking. And I couldn't even share you with her and Jack."

"What do you mean 'share me'? I was your adopted daughter. There was never any question about that."

"But we cut off all contact. We said it was for your sake because you were too young to deal with death. But it was really because I couldn't share you."

The sunrise is complete now, and the sky looks bright and clear. No snowstorm today? No volleyball team at school to beat us up, except for Kierstead. No walk along the track necessary? Maybe the fortune cookie's different plan does include a longer life. My heart double beats with hope.

I lean over and hug Mom tight, feeling her bones against me. "I love you."

"I love you, too."

I hug her some more, and my body feels curiously lighter. When we let go of each other, I smile, feeling open like that sky outside. Maybe all those family secrets clouded our horizon for too long. For the first time, I look at Mom without feeling angry. "I think you were meant to be my mother right from the moment I was conceived. It was destiny."

Mom smiles back. "All things considered, you must be right."

Dad joins us and we enjoy our granola and chia seed cereal together. "Looks like the meteorologists were wrong about that storm they predicted. It's a perfect clear day."

Predictions can be wrong, fate can change. *If it doesn't snow, maybe I can live.*

Only outside the window, I now spot one feather-like flake drifting to the ground.

"Anyway, we'll shut down early if it does turn into a storm. You should come straight home, too, Paige," Mom says.

Coming straight home, that could work. I wouldn't be on the track at the same time as before. "Yes. I won't volunteer at the library today."

We all head out together, like so many other times in our life. But this may be the last time for me. I hug them both and blink back tears. As the van drives off, I wave till I can't see them anymore. I will miss our daily routine. I will miss them, my family, crazy mixed-up and mismatched as we are. If I can't make fate budge for me, I will miss life.

I walk a few blocks and meet up with Jasmine.

As we stroll toward school, I tell her about our dinner at the Mandarin and the plans being made for a two-family trip to China. I also explain about the kidney transplant.

A few more feathers of snow drift down. A chill runs up my spine.

"Wow, your mom is a brave lady."

"Maybe she's too tough for her own good. Kim's mom seems to have recovered and gotten on with her life." I stop and glance at Jazz. *If I have to die, I need to save her.* That's why I came back. Helping Jazz will make up for the best friend . . . sister I couldn't help. "Did you explain to your mom about Cameron?"

"I tried. But she's not hearing me. She calls Cameron a cake boy. Cripes, it was Max who baked the cream puffs." She marches along quickly.

The snow feathers perform pirouettes, now. My heart sinks. The weather is playing out exactly the same as my last death day.

"Secrets weigh you down, Jazz." To save her, I need to convince her. "I didn't even know my family had any. But I feel so much better now understanding everything about Kim."

"Yeah?" She looks at me.

"I can't cover for you today. I promised my mom I would head straight home. 'Cause of the storm."

"Oh, come on. I need you. I don't get to see Cameron at all on Sunday."

"Bring Cameron to my house after school. I'll ask Max, too."

"What if Mom spots us?"

"She thinks he's safe, remember? You have to wear your parents down on the dating thing. You have to, Jazz. Promise me."

"Okay, okay! Here come Cameron and Max."

Thankfully they're both agreeable to hanging with us at my house. So I've managed to change our school leaving time. And nothing can make me take that shortcut along the track again. There will be four of us walking together, one of us being the love of Vanessa's life. Surely she won't beat us up in front of Cameron if she still has feelings for him.

We head off for our separate classes. In English, we finish *Romeo and Juliet*. Mrs. Corbin reads the last scene out loud to us. You can tell she loves Shakespeare and she makes me love it, too. But Romeo and Juliet still die in the end.

I feel sick.

When the bell rings, I wait till everyone leaves. "I just want to say, Mrs. Corbin, that I never liked English class until you taught it."

"My goodness. Thank you, Paige."

"You're welcome." I smile and leave. As I step into the hall, someone bumps into me, shoving me into the wall.

"Good work, Banana." Kierstead puts her face right close to mine, and I swear I can smell smoke on her breath, the liar. "You killed the volleyball team. After school, I'm gonna kill you."

Those words. Will she be my new fate, my new death?

I stand up to her, anyway. If things can't be changed, why should I cower?

"Kierstead, even if you kill every girl at school, Cameron's not gonna go out with you."

She steps back. "What are you talking about? He's Van's boyfriend."

"You knew that was over, didn't you? He just felt sorry for her. He was itching for someone new."

"Shut up." She rams me against the wall and heads off.

Max runs over. "What did you say this time?"

"I was hoping to persuade Kierstead to leave Jazz alone. But it didn't go well."

He loops his arm through mine. "No career in diplomacy for you."

Later, in gym class, Mrs. Brown asks me if I want to play on the volleyball team. A few spots have opened up.

I grin, still hopeful, and answer, "Sure."

But the snow starts coming down harder at noon and buries the streets by second break. For that lunch, I eat poutine at Max's suggestion. "It's got all your fat needs for the week in one meal," he tells me.

It will have to satisfy my fat needs for my lifetime. My last lunch on death row. I like the salty gravy. And the texture of the melted cheddar over the softening fries.

Someone is watching me, though. I can feel the eyes. I whip around and see Kierstead, her face screwed up as she stares.

I give her the finger.

She winks.

We arrive at French class at the same time, but I notice she's texting on her phone right from start to dismissal. I will Madame Potvin to notice. But she doesn't.

"Your attention, please," Mrs. Norr's voice sputters to life over the intercom. "The school will be closing at dismissal due to the storm. No library, gym or Environment Club."

With Kierstead's texting, the former volleyball team has to know that we're leaving the school at 3:15 sharp today, although they can't be certain of our route. On the bright side, there is nothing smeared on anyone's locker.

D-day Afternoon

∞

Max and I dress as warmly as we can. He even picks up a hat from Lost and Found.

"Oooh. You'll get lice."

"Over frostbite and amputated ears, I'll take bugs."

We meet Jazz and Cameron at his locker. I feel I should at least warn them about Kierstead's texting. I won't need to use prior knowledge of those Facebook plans I saw the last time I lived through this day. But when I tell them, neither seems to take it all that seriously.

"Really, what are they gonna do?" Cameron asks as we head for the door. "There are two guys with you, don't forget."

"Oh, against ten girls? You figure that's an even playing field?" Jazz says.

Max pushes open the door, and the wind blasts snow up against us.

"Maybe we'll get lucky." I raise my voice over the wind. "How can anyone see anything in weather like this?"

"Anybody got any money? We could grab a cab," Jazz suggests loudly.

"No," Max says. "Happy engagement to Beena, remember?"

"I've got five bucks. That's not enough for bus fare, is it?" I ask.

Jazz shakes her head. "One of my uncles is a bus driver. He'll tell my parents. Let's just walk along the tracks. It's quicker, anyhow."

The tracks.

She's right, waiting for the bus might take forever. Still. How is the storm affecting the train's schedule? Can we predict when one will come? I swallow hard as we struggle through the drifts and wind. "On one condition," I announce.

"What?" Jazz asks.

"I don't care how deep the snow is on either side, none of you are walking on the actual track. Okay?"

"Safety first," Max chuckles.

"Laugh all you want. Trains can't stop like cars. And in the storm, we won't hear them coming."

"You're being ridiculous. Let's just go."

The four of us squeeze together across the sidewalk, with Max trailing half on, half off. The wind moans high and then low like a siren as it flings snow in our faces. I hook one arm around Max's elbow, the other around Jasmine's. Together we stumble through it.

Before even reaching the intersection, we turn off the block, and I have to let go of them so they can climb over the chain-link fence.

"I don't think this is a good idea," I say.

"C'mon, just do it." Max takes my backpack from me, but it's impossible to jam my toe in the diamond of wire to start the climb.

"Here." Max bends a little, cupping his hands to provide a ladder step for me.

I step on his palms quickly, and he lifts as I fling one leg, then the other, over the top. Then I let go and drop hard on the ground.

Jazz lands an instant after, and the guys throw the backpacks to us. Cameron scrambles over, no problem, but Max with his wide feet has the same trouble as I did.

"Take your boots off," I suggest.

"Or you'll have to go around," Jazz says.

Max shakes his head but pitches his boots over to us. He winces as he squeezes his toes in the wire holes, foot by foot. Then he's over, too, shoving his wet feet back into his boots.

We pick up our backpacks and start the hike along the snowbank, two of us at either side of the tracks. I keep looking back and trying to make out sounds, even though we should be perfectly safe on these banks. A few steps along, Jazz sinks up to her knees and, when she hoists her foot up, her boot comes off. "This is ridiculous; we're walking there. It's been plowed." Cameron helps her get out of the snow and, with her boot back on, they start to walk down the center of the track.

"No, no, you can't!" Despite the cold, my face heats up like it's on fire. I hold my head in my hands.

"Why are you so worried?" Max asks gently, taking one hand away.

I can't say anything for a moment. Even if the rules didn't forbid me from warning anyone based on knowledge gained from the last take of this week, no one would believe me. I take a breath. "Because I had a nightmare about this."

"Okay. Well, I'll keep walking with you here, then." He speaks softly as though he's trying to calm a little kid.

Whatever. I want Jazz and Cameron off the track, too. I came back this week to stand up for her, to save her, and I thought we had a deal. But they're already too far ahead for me to argue with them. As we trudge on, hoisting our feet up and over the snow, I feel my body get hotter and my energy drain. We're a warehouse building away from the overpass when I get stuck right up to mid-thigh. I fling myself backward and blow the bangs from my eyes. I want to melt into the cold snow.

Max grabs my arm and pulls, up and up. He forces me to climb out. "Look. We'll walk on the track; it will be fine. Dreams are just dreams," he says.

"You don't understand. We won't be able to get off in time."

"I'll walk backward. I'll watch out for the rest of us," Max says.

"No. That won't work." He does have a good idea, though. "It has to be me. I won't be able to walk unless I personally know at all times that there is no train coming."

"Okay."

Both of us step up to the snow-covered gravel between the two metal rails. I look toward the overpass. A short walk home that is going to take forever, if I even make it home at all.

Max holds my hand as I stumble sideways, always squinting to make out that all-important train headlight, always listening to identify random sounds.

"I think that's them!" Jazz calls back to us.

I face forward and peer in the direction she points. Five bodies shuffle up the overpass. Five against four, way better odds than ten against one or even two. Will they really wait there in the storm for us? Maybe that's why there are only five of them. Five on first watch, while the others hang around in the doughnut shop warming up for the next shift.

"Just keep going. Hurry!" I tell her.

Cameron and Jazz run, and the figures climbing the overpass don't seem to notice us.

But then I feel the rumble under my feet, thunder from the ground. I hear the long and short wail of the horn. Through the falling white, I make out the lone round headlight.

The train catches the attention of the figures on the top of the overpass, too, and when they look down to see the train, they also spot us.

"There they are!" Kierstead's voice yells. "Let's get 'em!"

Four of them begin running down the overpass, but one person stays at the top. Her hands grab the railing.

"Get off the track, Jazz. Cameron. Max!" I wave my arm and they jump to one side instantly. I step back into the high snow with Max. Deep snow and all, we begin running.

The person on the overpass hoists herself up, one leg over, then the other.

No!

The figure drops down like a sack of cement. She lands on her feet but falls to her side across the track.

"Vanessa, get up!" I scream.

The train howls short and long again.

All she has to do is roll over a couple of times. She raises her head. I see her hazel eyes. They look dead.

Vanessa doesn't move.

There are only a couple of heartbeats of time in which you get to decide to do things and then you can regret what you don't do for an eternity. I think I can change my fate but maybe I just can't, not without taking out someone else instead of me.

I scramble back onto the track and reach for Vanessa. My hands connect with her back and I shove as hard as I can, which means her body moves. *Far enough?* I have about a second to wonder. Mine has moved, too, though. I feel the hot wind from the engine and scream as I try to throw myself to the side. Something impacts with my head. Hard. Like a rocket. Everything in front of me shatters into white and gold shards. Nothing hurts, though. There is no blackness.

Back at the Beach

∞

I blink a few times, clearing my eyes of the excess liquid. I inhale deeply and make out the white snow. Strangely, it feels hot against my face. I roll to my feet and stand up.

"You're back." It's Kim's voice. My sister. The sun glows around her silhouette.

I blink again and realize the snow is actually sand. No boots on my feet anymore. I wiggle my toes, and the hot sugary texture feels nice. Of course, this all means that my real body is lying on that hospital bed. "For a little while back there, I thought I could beat death," I tell her, discouraged.

"You did a great thing back there." Kim smiles at me. She seems a lot happier than the previous two times I saw her. "You didn't owe that witch anything."

I nod. "Vanessa is easy to hate. But I saw her eyes and felt sorry, too, you know?"

"You care about people more." Kim's voice sounds warmer than before.

"Did I save her?" I ask.

"From the train, yes." Kim tilts her head, and I see her bottom lip fold.

"Are you saying Vanessa is just going to commit suicide some other time, when I'm not around?" I ask.

"I can't tell the future," Kim says. "But she's in the hospital with you. She'll get psychiatric counseling. Mrs. Norr knows about her problems with her mother. She has a way better chance than I did with the *E. coli*." Kim's smile droops.

"Oh, Kimmee, I would have given anything to save you."

Her head bows so that her chin touches her chest.

"If they had let me, I would have given you my kidney. I would have gone to India to do it. You know I would have."

"Yes, but you don't get that choice right now." Her voice sounds sad and tired.

I reach out and hug her. Solid flesh, exactly like my own. Her hair on the back of my arm feels silky, her back bony. She is beautiful, though. Am I that beautiful? Uncle Jack and Aunt Bev think so. Max, too.

She hugs me tightly.

I see her tears and feel my own.

"You don't want to be with me, do you?" she asks gently.

"Why? What is it, Kim? Is Mom never going to let me go? Do you have to go on without me?"

Kim shrugs.

"I told Mom and Dad I wanted them to give away my organs. If I'm brain-dead, they should be taking those away soon."

Saying nothing, Kim turns and walks toward the ocean.

"What more can I do?" I feel her sorrow, heavy like an anchor. She has been lonely, just like me. For seven years she has missed me, too.

She beckons with her hand to follow.

I walk slowly after her, into the icy water that stings with salt.

"See?" she says as she moves her fingers in the water.

I look down and feel myself drifting and drifting.

Between Two Worlds

∞

When I can focus again, I see four beige cinder-block walls around me. *Where am I?*

Ahead of me I see my mother sitting hunched over a body on a bed, holding a hand, my hand, and talking. "You listen to me. You need to wake up. You're too young to die. There's no reason for this."

"I'm with Kimberly now," I say. "I'm with my sister. Let me go. Give away my kidney." My vision of the room fades and I see Kim.

"Sis?" She holds out her hand. "Come with me. Let's go exploring." She smiles, showing those perfect straight teeth I had to wear braces for three years to achieve.

I reach out. But then I hear my mother start to cry. Her pain tears at my heart. I want to do just about anything to comfort her.

"Stop being so stubborn!" I yell at Mom, and the vision

of Kim fades to that hospital room again. "I'm dead. We didn't even try to save Kim. Let's save somebody else at least!"

Mom sobs harder. I move forward and wrap my arms around her shoulders. "I love you, Mom," I whisper. "I wish I had been born to you, wish I looked like you. Wish I could grow up to be like you."

"If you can hear me, squeeze my hand," she begs.

"It's no use, Mom. I'm not in there." I try to pick up her other hand and squeeze it. Nothing.

"All right. You can't squeeze my hand. At least blink your eyes. If you can blink your eyes, you can come back to me. You just have to want to come back to me, Paige. Paige, try!"

She makes me want to come back more than anything else. I would hold Max's hand again, enjoy his kisses, watch him grow tall and handsome. I would score more volleyball serves, I would graduate from high school, I would help Jazz reason with her parents so we could study biology in university together. Eat every kind of food in the world. Visit China, maybe even India.

Something starts to pull at me, like some kind of vacuum cleaner inside of me tugging me this way and that. "My best friend, my sister!" I say.

"Go ahead, blink your eyes if you want to," Kim says sadly from somewhere behind me.

My eyes feel heavy just then, but I struggle. "Kimmee?"

She comes back into focus.

I throw my arms around her. "I love you, Kim, and I'd give anything to have you back in my life."

"Please, Paige." Mom's voice.

"But you don't have life if you choose to be with me," Kim interrupts. Her voice drops. "You love your mother more."

"In an entirely different way." I shrug my shoulders. "I'm so sorry, Kim. I feel more connected to her."

Kim's head hangs down. "But we're blood related. Our DNA is exactly the same."

"Will you always be here for me, no matter when I die?" I ask.

She places one hand over her heart and reaches the other hand out to mine. I place my hand over it.

"Blink your eyes, Paige," my mother calls. "You can do it."

I let my lids drop and squeeze tightly. "Good-bye, Kim." I feel everything inside me get sucked away. Suddenly, I can move nothing except my eyelids. I blink them again.

"Good-bye, Paige." I hear a voice as if from the end of a long passageway in my head.

"Paige, you did it!" Mom yells.

Every muscle, every bone, every pore pulses with pain.

"Doctor, nurse! Come quickly, she's back! My baby came back to me!"

I try to smile, but don't think my lips lift. *See you later, Kim!* I send that thought back to my sister.

Another time, another place, I won't be able to sidestep death, and then I will be with her again. Will we both be young with smooth skin and long hair? Or will we have gray hair and wrinkles? Will someone be able to use the parts of my body? Who knows? It will depend on the choices I make and the hand fate deals me. For now, I take a deep, labored breath. I need to work on getting better so that I can live out the rest of my life.

THE END